ELEMENTAL FACTORS

NEUTRINOMAN AND LIGHTNINGIRL: A LOVE STORY,
EPISODE 6

ROBERT J. MCCARTER

LITTLE HUMMINGBIRD PUBLISHING

Elemental Factors

Neutrinoman and Lightningirl: A Love Story, Episode 6

Cover image: 123rf.com/profile_kesu87

Version 1.0, June 2020

ISBN: 978-1-941153-40-6

Find out more about this series at: Neutrinoman.com

Visit Robert's website at: RobertJMcCarter.com

Published by:

Little Hummingbird Publishing

P.O. Box 23518

Flagstaff, AZ 86002

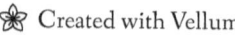 Created with Vellum

NEUTRINOMAN & LIGHTNINGIRL: A LOVE STORY

- Meteor Attack!
- Toxic Asset
- Protocol X
- Season 1 (Omnibus edition of Episodes 1 - 3)
- Off Book
- Hard Times
- Elemental Factors
- Season 2 (Omnibus edition of Episodes 4-6, coming August , 2020)

Find out the latest at Neutrinoman.com

1 / NERVES

I WAS AN ONLY CHILD. I HAD GREAT PARENTS. I WAS CURIOUS and loved to tinker with things and take them apart, spending hours at this not even aware if someone was with me or not. You'd think that being alone wouldn't be that big of a deal for me, but the thought of going into the conference room was terrifying. I'd much rather face down aliens bent on our destruction or go up against Toxicwasteman.

I am Nik Nichols, aka Neutrinoman, I've saved the world a couple of times now but am afraid of a bunch of military brass and suits in a conference room.

I was standing there fidgeting while Licia was looking at me with those soulful brown eyes of hers, so full of compassion, and it's frankly hard for me to meet that gaze. We were standing in a nondescript hallway with short brown carpet and bright fluorescent lights. Down the hall I could see a window and a slice of the orderly streets of Phoenix, Arizona, with the craggy humps of Camelback Mountain beyond. The air-conditioning was humming, the circulating air playing with some of the fine black hairs framing Licia's round face and escaping her ponytail.

"You got this, honey," she said, touching my arm, a brief spark of our q-morph powers flowing between us. She stepped close and fiddled with my tie and smoothed the lapel of the suit jacket I was wearing, and I'm grateful that I don't have to meet those eyes.

Before September 10, 2003, when the cosmic rays hit and the power plant melted down and the rat bit me and I was transformed into Neutrinoman, I was a janitor working at the Palo Verde Nuclear Generating Station. Back then I was still finding myself, still fairly aimless and drifting along, working a low-paying job just so I could see the inside of a nuclear power plant. Back then you'd swear I was fine being alone, that I even enjoyed it.

I swallowed, trying to smile at Licia, my eyes flicking to the conference room door and then back down the hallway, wishing I was a janitor right now, not a superhero, and certainly not *this* superhero.

At Palo Verde, as a janitor, I was always moving, sweeping, polishing floors, taking the garbage out. It's not like you weren't alone walking down those large halls, hearing the slap of your feet on the polished cement echo through the large spaces, hauling garbage out into the Phoenix heat, looking around the flat, sandy landscape as the desert sucked the moisture out of you. Sure you saw people, but only for brief interludes.

"How're the kids, Frank?"

"Oh great, Nik. Little Fran's birthday is next week. Did you see the Steelers game on Sunday?"

"Sure did, the old man and I barbequed, tinkered with the Charger."

Simple interactions. Not that intimate, not when looked at one at a time. Just moments here and there. But you stack them up and you get to know someone, you can see their faces sagging when they've had a bad day, or their eyes bright when things are going good.

And I guess before Homeland Security arrested me, threw me into that hole for two hundred days, tried to break me by isolating me, I didn't think much about it. Being alone, that is.

As a janitor I had frequent interactions, I had the huge spaces of Palo Verde to wander through. I walked miles in a shift and wasn't locked in a cell walking around and around just for something to do.

As Neutrinoman I had spent a good amount of time off the planet, either in orbit, or farther out when I went after the earth-killing meteor that the aliens sent our way.

But I was never alone for long.

I saw other faces frequently.

I interacted with other humans all the time.

Try being locked in a cell with no human interaction, no smartphone, no internet, no books.

Well, there were a couple of books and Ronald, the kind man that brought them to me. Except he wasn't really there, a q-morph sent by Tom Tyree (Toxicwasteman) that could project his presence and the books he gave to me into my mind. He was there to keep me sane.

And he did.

But barely.

Back in that hallway, I took a deep breath and let it come rushing out, blowing more of those stray black hairs on Licia's head. The past, that imprisonment and all that happened around my release is haunting me. It keeps coming back to me.

She looked up and did her best to smile, but I knew her well enough to know it was not a real smile. Things have changed since we met and saved the earth from that meteor, since the aliens tried to kill me and Tom Tyree tried to recruit me, since Gaia destroyed the Hoover Dam, and since they locked me up.

It's not like I was going to be alone in that room. But... well... I wasn't going to have Licia by my side, and that now feels like being alone. She's been with me most every moment since I got out of that prison, since I fought the q-morph soldier, since we ran off to Mexico and agreed to start Heroes Incorporated.

I didn't used to be like this.

"It's going to be okay," she said, pulling me into a fierce hug. "You have to face them, you know this. And they have to listen to you."

I couldn't speak, I just nodded.

"You're my man, my Neutrinoman," she whispered.

"And you're my girl, my Lightningirl," I whispered back.

She loved me, I know she did, but I needed her too much. How long would she stick with the needy, afraid to be without her, version of me.

I took a deep breath, trying to still my mind, slip back into the meditation routine I started in prison, but it just wasn't working.

"I know it will be okay," I whispered back, telling her the lie we both needed to hear.

She let me go and I turned and walked into that conference room.

2 / A PLAN

Licia had a plan.

Our world had fallen apart, our life in exile in the high desert of central Arizona vaporized, and my amazing wife had a plan.

And I had no idea. I was completely clueless.

After the war with the aliens, after all the madness, the Quantum Metamorph Accord of 2020 had separated us surviving q-morphs, hiding us away from the public, keeping us isolated. And our home had been Casita de Soledad. And the military had planted a bomb under us they called "Project Vulcan," and after I learned about it, I hadn't been able to live with it.

Project Vulcan, and my insistence on poking at it, had literally blown our home and our life up. There was nothing left of Casita de Soledad, just a perfectly spherical void in the ground, everything in the blast radius vaporized... nearly the both of us with it.

I kept seeing it, that spherical void in the ground where our home used to be. Bushes and trees on the edge sliced cleanly, inside the sphere, the ground smooth and a bit shiny like the explosion had polished it. A void where our home used to be, where our lives used to be.

I had hated our small pedestrian life, railed at the limitations, hated how Homeland Security kept us there, watched us, chided us when we used our powers. We had battled the Arcturian Alliance. We had saved the world over and over, and we had become their pet superheroes sent out to the high desert of central Arizona just in case we were needed again. Project Vulcan had been their insurance in case we got out of control.

And, I guess that is what I did... I lost control and brought this on us.

"They... I..." I mumbled as we trudged over the high Arizona desert naked and barefoot. We had both transformed to our quantum forms during the explosion—the only way we could survive—we had no clothes left to wear. Gone was my giddy laughter of relief right after survival. Reality had settled in on me. I had been in prison once after that mess with Gaia at the Hoover Dam, where they tried to break me through extreme isolation, and I suspected it would be worse if they caught us this time.

The sun was rushing down to the horizon, casting the cactus, sage brush, and brown wild grasses in a warm light that didn't cheer me like it usually did. The heat of the day would soon bleed off leaving us naked, hungry, and still running.

Anger was coming, brewing just below the surface, but not there yet. It was trapped like that super volcano under Yellowstone the aliens tried to get me to activate.

I was confused and lost trudging through the desert, walking around cactus and yucca on my battered feet, only barely aware that my beautiful wife was nude in front of me, but quite aware that she didn't seem nearly as heartbroken as I and wasn't loudly yelping at each bump and scrape to her feet.

She had a plan.

Her spine was erect, her shoulders squared, her long black hair sliding over her shoulders as she walked, her steady rhythm nearly metronomic.

"I can't believe they did that... I..." I continued to mumble, barely above a whisper. I was exhausted, I had depleted myself saving us from the explosion—or vaporization. Really, a better word for it.

The desert revealed itself slowly as the hills rose and fell under our feet, covered in dead grasses, prickly pear cactus, sage brush, and yucca plants with their sharp needlelike leaves here and there. It was beautiful land, land that I loved, but I wasn't feeling it.

We were in the high desert of central Arizona a few miles east of I-17, but Licia had us heading north. The direction didn't make any sense to me. To the west was I-17 and the possibility of help, and to the east was the high-tension powerlines that carried electricity to Flagstaff. Even though they had been severed where Casita de Soledad used to be, there might be power there to the south.

But she was walking north. With intent and purpose.

Homeland Security would be looking for us. We cleared their hidden base out before I triggered the bomb, so they know what happened. Although, since we barely survived, they must know there is a good chance that we were vaporized in the blast along with every single one of our possessions, along with the adobe house and greenhouses we had built ourselves, along with our lives that were small and boring, but comfortable and simple.

The summer evening was warm, a slight breeze licking the sweat off my bare skin, but I barely noticed as my mind went over what had happened, as that anger got closer to the surface. My foot landed on part of a decaying piece of prickly pear cactus. It was a dull brown and faded green, blending in with the sandy soil, and I hadn't seen it.

"Damn!" I cried, hopping on one foot while I raised the other and tried to yank it out. It was old and half decomposed, the once bright skin of the cactus now dull and flaking, bits of its harder skeletal structure a lattice visible through breaks in the skin. The needles were a tawny color, three long ones and many of the hair-like smaller ones embedded in my foot.

I hopped, I pulled at the cactus, and all I managed to do was come down on another piece of the decaying cactus with my other foot.

I fell hard to the ground, landing on some old grass. The grass broke my fall, but it also poked my bare behind in some very uncomfortable places. I just sat there, both feet lifted watching Licia walk away.

It was no use. I had flown us, low and fast, about a mile before my energy faded, before Licia and I had to surrender our quantum forms and become entirely flesh and blood. Homeland Security would be here any moment, but we were naked, we had nothing, and I couldn't even walk.

And yet she kept walking, her spine straight, her stride steady. She didn't even look back.

Licia had a plan and nothing was going to stop her, not even my little cactus mishap.

She didn't speak, she didn't encourage me, she just kept walking. And I knew that walk, that posture, she was furious. Definitely at Homeland because of the bomb, maybe at me for not letting things be, probably at the world for putting such a burden on us and then discarding us.

I smiled, just a tiny bitter little smile, as I watched her and thought those things. That's what *I* was mad about, that's what *I* was feeling. I've been married long enough to know it's not a good idea to project your own emotional state and foibles on your spouse. I'm sure Licia was feeling many things, and having known her for so long, I could guess that anger was primary, but it was best to let her tell me what she was feeling. But she wasn't talking, only walking.

But there it was, that spark of anger, some energy, something I could use.

I took a deep breath and let it out slowly focusing on my feet and the decaying cacti embedded there. I dug deep, like I had learned I could do all those years ago after I got out of prison and had to battle the q-morph soldier. The bottom of my feet glowed yellow, taking on the neutrino swirls. Not long, just for a moment, just enough to burn out the needles, and I let it go.

I stood up and took a deep breath and started walking after my wife.

I now had a plan, follow Licia, learn how she plans to get us to that interview with Diane Madison, do whatever it takes to make that happen.

But even below that, guiding that short-term plan was another plan. A simple plan. A one world plan.

Licia.

My love, my life, together we would figure this out, and if not, we would fight and we would fall, but together.

3 / A FREE AGENT

THE CONFERENCE ROOM DOOR CLICKED LOUDLY BEHIND ME and I did my best not to jump, sweat slowly trickling down my neck despite the excessive air-conditioning.

I felt Licia's absence. It felt like an ache that wouldn't go away, like I wouldn't be all right until she was by my side again.

The conference room was on the twentieth floor of an office building in downtown Phoenix. This floor was used by the US Department of Housing and Urban Development. Not military, not police, but government. Fairly neutral ground.

Out the floor-to-ceiling windows, I saw the flat grid of the city laid out, the north-south, east-west flow only interrupted by the small craggy protrusions of the desert that rose up in rounded humps. Hunks of tan rock that reminded me of Gaia and her ability to control the earth, like how she turned a sandstone canyon into a giant rock monster and destroyed the Hoover Dam.

That destruction is what got me "detained" and what ended up putting me here. It wasn't lost on me that Tom Tyree (Toxicwaste-man) had lured me to Vegas to try to capture Chaosboy, had sent me out to the dam to confront Gaia, had been instrumental in that "detainment." (Not to mention Ronald who got me through it fairly intact.)

The people sitting at the conference table were waiting for me, I could hear the squeak of chairs, the rustle of papers, and a few low sighs. The room stank of fear and not just my own.

"Thank you for coming, Nik."

It was Colonel Williams speaking. I would recognize that gravel in his voice anywhere.

I had my hands behind my back as I stood in front of the long conference room table, hopeful it seemed like a confident gesture and they didn't know I was clenching those hands. I could see them out of my peripheral vision, but I was still staring out at the window at the cars crawling below.

"Would you like to sit?" he asked.

I let my eyes focus on them. Colonel Williams was at the head of the table in a crisp blue dress uniform, his green eyes boring into me. Around the table were other men and women, some in military uniforms, a few in suits. I spotted a general, but not General Markus, which was one of the conditions of this meeting. I smiled, they looked more nervous than I did, the sharp scent of the nervous sweat clear to my rat-enhanced sense of smell.

"Thank you, Colonel Williams," I said, "but this won't take very long."

A thin woman in a dark blue skirt and jacket cleared her throat. She was in her fifties, her wrinkles and her tight ponytail giving her an elegant feel. "On behalf of the president," she began, "I would like to convey our nation's eternal gratitude for your actions in defense of this country and our most sincere apology for what happened at the Groom Lake facility. Mr. Halifax clearly exceeded his authority on numerous occasions. His actions are most regrettable."

She was a powerful woman. You could tell by how she held herself amongst all the uniforms that surrounded her. Her spine was erect, her gaze steady, her hands folded neatly on the table. Melinda Michaels, the Secretary of State, I hadn't expected anyone of her stature to be at this meeting.

"Did the president know of this facility and its intent?" I asked her, my insides quivering but my voice strong.

She nodded sharply. "Yes, he did."

I took a deep breath, my eyes leaving her and going back to that window, back to that view that confirmed I wasn't locked up, that I could jump out that window, turn into Neutrinoman, and fly away.

"I appreciate your honesty, Madam Secretary," I said, still not looking at her, "but perhaps you will understand that his apology feels political, not genuine." I turned back to her. "You, too, I assume, knew of the facility and its intent."

She nodded, pursing her lips.

"Honesty," I said. "This is a good start. Let me return some honesty." I put my hands on the back of the chair I had been meant to sit in, high backed and faux leather. I squeezed it as hard as I could without it looking obvious. I thought of throwing it through the window, letting in the hot dry air, making my escape route that much easier. "Let me tell you what Mr. Halifax so desperately wanted to know," I said. "Let me treat you all with the respect you have never shown me."

I licked my lips and almost didn't do it, didn't tell the truth, but I was tired of hiding. "I went to the Hoover Dam because Tom Tyree told me that Gaia was targeting it. I chose not to inform the military because I feared a heavy hand would be used. I had a discussion with Tom *after* the breaking of the Hoover Dam in which he encouraged me to feign chasing him so you all would go easier on me. I went to Las Vegas with Quinn Rask in the first place with the express purpose of capturing Chaosboy."

The room had gone silent, no more squeaking of chairs, no more sighs or coughs, all eyes were on me.

"And I was aided in your 'facility' by a q-morph sent by Tom who could project a convincing illusion of his presence into my mind. He's who I was talking to. It was through his power that I was reading books down there. He's the reason I held up so well."

Except it didn't feel to me like I held up well at all. I was sweating, surely they could see that. Surely they knew that I wanted to fly out of here, leave this planet with Licia and never return.

"Why are you telling us all of this?" Secretary Michaels asked.

I stopped, released my death grip on the chair and stood up tall. "Because I won't, under any circumstances, work directly for the United States government again. I'm sure you know about Heroes Incorporated. We are moving forward with it. Any future dealings you have with q-morphs that are part of our consortium will be through a negotiated legal contract. We will be treated fairly. We will not be kept in the dark. We will be partners not weapons you deploy at a whim."

Williams gave me a single nod, he had been expecting this, but there were mumbles and movement and more squeaking chairs.

I gave it a few moments to settle down before continuing. "And I wanted to give you a complete account of what happened in Las Vegas in case you do deem my actions criminal. If so, then do arrest me, but do so in the light of day. Do imprison me, but do so humanely."

Secretary Michaels was talking, something about how things had gotten out of control at the "facility." The general was shooting questions at me and several other people were speaking. Williams was looking at me calmly, his eyes locked with mine, his lips turned up in the smallest of smiles.

"Two more things," I said loudly and waited until the voices had died down. "Colonel Williams will be the government's liaison with Heroes Incorporated." A bunch of mouths opened up to speak, but I held my hand up. "And, any q-morph prisoners in that 'facility' will be released. Immediately. Any crimes you deem that any of us have committed must be dealt with publicly and transparently. These points are *not* negotiable."

They were all looking at me, different people from different lives with a different view of what I was, what I could do, what kind of threat I posed to the country and the world. What kind of help I could provide. They saw me as a hero and villain both.

"You're worried about the Arcturian Alliance," I said slowly. "I am too. You don't know if you can trust me. I understand that and relate. I'm *quite* sure I can't trust you. You fear a single person having this much power. I do too. I fear how much power many of you wield. You are worried about Tom Tyree and what kind of influence he has had on me. I get that."

The room was eerily silent and they all stared at me again like I was a mind reader or something, but all of this stuff was totally obvious.

I took a deep breath and sighed, my shoulders slumping. "But I care about this planet and its people. I want us, as flawed as we are, to survive. And I believe you all feel the same way. So we must find a way to work together."

Secretary Michaels nodded, Williams smiled, there were some other nods and a few yeses and then I could see all the questions on their faces and my knees went weak. They wanted answers. They were hoping that I could provide them.

They were faking this just as much as I had been.

"I'm sure you're aware of what Heroes Incorporated is doing in Ruby, Arizona. I would consider it an act of good faith if you aided us in getting our base setup. It's remote so we need transportation help."

"Of course," Secretary Michaels said. Her mouth opened to say something else, but I cut her off.

"Then we are done for today. We'll reach out to Colonel Williams soon to coordinate."

I stood up straight, turned my back to them, and walked out the door. When it snapped shut behind me, my knees turned to water and I almost went down, but Licia was there and put her arm around me.

"Valentine has the car pulled up in front," she said gently. "We'll be out of Phoenix in no time."

I nodded and held tightly to her, feeling her electric tingle, drawing strength from her presence. Valentine Oscar was my bodyguard, he had appointed himself the role and would not accept payment for his services. He had been there when I got out of prison and had been essential to my recovery.

"We have a lot of work to do," I said, my voice barely above a whisper.

"Yes, we do," she answered.

4 / THE SECRET CAVE

THE CAVE WAS DARK, BUT LICIA WITH HER RAVEN-ENHANCED eyesight walked ahead of me like she knew exactly where she was going until the darkness swallowed her and I was left at the edge of the light, cool stone under my bare feet.

The air was damp in my nose and without clothing I began to quickly chill down. Our march across the desert had taken over an hour and the sun was setting and I had heard the sound of approaching helicopters right before we reached the cave.

We needed shelter, for sure, but we also needed food and water and a way to escape Homeland Security. And I needed power, either some potent radiation, or a lightning powerup from Licia.

As we marched over the desert, Licia's straight-backed determination had never wavered. She was quiet, her eyes fixed on a low hill with a craggy face. This hill. This cave. She had a plan.

We hadn't talked yet, my self-recriminations were so loud in my own head I didn't need any conversation. They clanged around having long conversations with my self-doubt with a few timely interjections by my self-loathing.

This was all me, my freak out caused all of this. I couldn't calmly confront Homeland Security after finding the bomb, Project Vulcan, after seeing just how closely they monitored us, after feeling that I was in prison all over again.

I took another sniff of the air and smelled feces, some kind of animal had lived in here, probably a rodent. And below that I could smell food, stale crackers maybe, and just a whiff of rust, like there was something metal back there.

A raven was involved in Licia's transformation into a q-morph, giving her that great eyesight, and a rat mine, giving me a discerning nose, and an obsession for cheese.

I heard the snick of metal against metal, items shifting around, and then light blossomed bright at the back of the cave.

Licia was standing there, the harsh bluish light from a small LED lantern illuminating her naked curves, making her light-brown skin look a tad blue. She stood in front of a metal footlocker that was about three feet wide and stuffed to the brim with gear.

My wife, she had a plan.

A secret plan.

One she hadn't breathed a word of to me.

My mind turned over sluggishly as I celebrated her forethought and cleverness, but also ground into the fact that she hadn't told me a thing. Not one word.

She was staring at me, a question on her face and then she blinked and nodded. "I'm sorry I didn't tell you," she said. She knew what I was thinking, decades together will do that. Or, rather, a decent emotional intelligence, which she certainly has, will do that.

I took a few tentative steps towards her. "I'm just glad you did," I said.

She bit her lip and sighed, her head slowly wagging back and forth, her long hair sliding across her bare back.

"I mean," I continued, it wasn't time for half-truths, "I *am* glad you did, but why didn't you tell me?"

She swallowed and nodded, and I knew she was sorting through her own feelings, which couldn't be easy in our current circumstance. She was trying to get to the core of it so she could satisfy me and we could move on. Quickly.

And I felt bad that I needed satisfying here, but I did.

"I didn't tell you..." she began, setting the lantern down and walking the few steps that separated us until she was standing right next to me. I could feel her heat, but I couldn't see her face very well, the lantern lighting her from behind, its rays a halo around her, reminding me of the goddess she becomes when she transforms into Lightningirl. "I didn't tell you because I was worried enough to do something but didn't want to believe that anything like this would happen."

I nodded. "I get that, but..."

"You were writing, lost in the past," she continued, her cool hand taking mine. "It was going well, doing you a lot of good. I... I didn't want to disturb that."

And there it was, my wife was looking towards the future while I had my head in the past, trying to get it all sorted out, both of us missing the present.

And the writing had done me a lot of good, to relive it, feel it again and then move on. But right then, in the cool and dusty cave, dirt and rocks under my feet, it twisted on me. Maybe if I hadn't been so busy writing, I could have done a better job of this. It was the writing that led to agreeing to the interview with Diane Madison, that had made Homeland nervous, got them thinking about using Project Vulcan. Nervous enough so that Colonel Williams got wind of it and came out and warned us. Maybe if the crushing weight of the war and all that happened along with the Quantum Metamorph Accord hadn't made me satisfied to be alone in the desert with my wife, this could have been different.

And then Licia was in my arms and she was shaking. From the cold, from how close we came to dying, from the seemingly insurmountable task in front of us, from all of that.

Her skin was cold against mine and I held her tight. I took a deep breath, a meditative one, and brought myself back to the present, using what I had learned in that prison below Groom Lake at Area 51. I took another deep breath and told Licia that I loved her, that she was all that mattered to me. And both were true. I listened to her telling me the same in her own words and let it feed me.

Her shaking stopped and I felt a strange warmth on my face coming from the back of the cave. Not much, just the tiniest bit as if the clouds had just broken on a cold and rainy day and a single shaft of light lanced out from the grey and found me. The feeling was familiar and I smiled.

"Is there some uranium back there?" I asked.

She nodded her head still buried in my chest.

"You are brilliant!" I exclaimed lifting her up and twirling her around. She must have taken some of our secret uranium stash and moved it here.

She giggled in that girlish way that just made my knees weak and I put her down and kissed her hard. At the very least I could fly us out of here, although that could get very complicated very quickly.

"So, we need to get to Diane Madison," I said, once our brief celebration was over.

"Yes. You said you can get us footage of what happened."

I nodded. "I need the internet, though."

She went back to the footlocker and rummaged around, and I wished I could stop the moment. We had a sliver of hope, like that sunbeam breaking through the clouds. I was a bit more myself and actually noticed how beautiful my petite, well-proportioned wife was, her movements graceful, her smile dazzling as she pulled a smartphone out of the footlocker and plugged in an external battery.

Hope, when you are truly feeling it, seems like it's going to last forever. The same is true for despair. Right then it seemed like we could do this, it seemed like that feeling would last forever, but nothing does, does it?

I couldn't make the moment last, but I did savor it, did breathe it, steeling myself for the fight I knew would come next.

5 / A TORNADO

FALL 2006, PHOENIX, ARIZONA

Timothy Tran had this way of walking that would make you think he either worked out all the time, drank way too much coffee, or both. He was short, maybe five-eight, with a compact, athletic body, and he liked to pace. All the time.

"The name is stupid," he shot off with such conviction it seemed like the statement was meant to end the conversation. He was wearing grey sweats and a Missouri Tigers T-shirt. He had jet-black hair with just a few grey invaders visible.

But it was his eyes that caught you. His irises were so dark you couldn't tell where they ended and his pupils started. When he looked at you, it felt like he was looking through you, into another world or something.

Licia and I sat at the small round table in his hotel room in Birmingham, Alabama, while he paced the short stretch between the door to the hotel room and the bathroom door, looking like he was going to wear a path in the uninspired grey carpet.

The room was messy, books and papers covering one of the two beds, the other bed had his suitcase on it with the clothing spilling out. There was room enough for him to sleep, but it was easy to believe that he never bothered with such things. The room stank of old takeout Chinese food and cigarettes.

"Sorry," Licia said with a smile, her arms crossed over her sweater like she was mad or cold or both. "The name Heroes Incorporated comes with the funding." It was damp, the patter of rain and the dripping of the gutter outside a constant white noise.

Licia hadn't wanted to come along on these recruiting missions, finding q-morphs to join Heroes Incorporated. I hadn't begged. We hadn't fought. I just told her that I needed her.

And I did.

I was having nightmares almost every night. Being alone—and at this point that meant being without Licia—left me prone to panic attacks.

"We need you," I said to Timothy when his restless course brought him close and his eerie dark eyes briefly connected with mine. He stopped, brushed his overlong black bangs back away from his face, gave me a sharp nod and continued to pace.

It seemed that was easy for him to imagine, that we needed him, but the question seemed to be, did he need us?

He stopped at an open laptop on his bed and poked at the keyboard briefly. It showed a map of the area with radar information overlaid in garish colors. He was a storm chaser and the q-morph known as Tornado. In 2003 when the cosmic rays hit, he was caught by a class-five tornado, his truck, with him in it, swept up in its embrace. He had gotten too close, the tornado had caught him.

Earlier, when he had told us about it, he had stopped his pacing, his eyes wide, his body still, his mouth open just a bit, his hand brushing at the tuft of black hair under his lip. "For a moment," he had said, his voice reverent, "it was perfect. I was weightless. I was in the storm. I *was* the storm. Time seemed to stop."

He had blinked and sighed.

"And then?" Licia had prompted.

"And then..." he shrugged. "My head slammed into the window and the next thing I knew I woke up naked, not a scratch on me, in the wake of the tornado's destruction with these weird eyes." He pointed at his black orbs, shrugged, and resumed his pacing.

After we had shared our transformation stories, after I told him just a bit about my "detainment" and the prison made for q-morphs, we had pitched him "Heroes Incorporated" and asked him to leave the military and join us. And all we had gotten was him telling us that the name was stupid.

And he had a point, but not a point that mattered.

"We're setting up a base in southern Arizona not far from the Mexico border," I said, trying to figure out what this guy wanted, what would entice him. That location, so close to another country, was important to me.

His lips took on a brief snarl. "Desert," he spit out, his pacing not slowing down.

Licia caught my eye, her eyebrows raising slightly. "It's just the base. The word is out about Heroes Incorporated. We are getting interest in your services from some exotic locations."

I nodded. "Retainer clients for hurricane season. Puerto Rico, Cuba, Hawaii. Florida."

"Hurricanes? They want me... I..." His pacing finally stopped and his normally barely-there accent thickened. Timothy was born in South Korea but moved to the United States with his family when he was seven.

Licia smiled. "Yes. Hurricanes. We don't expect you can absorb enough energy to stop them, but you should be able to blunt them, maybe tweak their course."

The military had him down here hoping to find a tornado even though it was fall not summer. In my mind they were doing it for two reasons, so he could power up if possible, and to keep him busy. He was horribly underused, we wanted to find out if he could do more.

If he could... well, this was important. He could save lives and give Heroes Incorporated a good stream of income.

"There's a class three hurricane approaching Puerto Rico," I said. "We can get you there with a team to support you. A ship, a plane, whatever you need."

"We can get you there, tonight," Licia added.

His eyes wide, Timothy Tran, the Tornado, smiled.

6 / TWEET TWEET

I TOOK THE CHEAP SMARTPHONE FROM MY WIFE AND MOVED to the entrance of the cave. We had a good line of sight, the Mogollon Rim unseen behind us, the rolling hills of our former home spread out to the south. Low hills covered in cactus and the dried grasses of summer, with the cut of I-17 visible here and there to the west. The sun, low on the horizon, was turning up the contrast with the western faces of the hills a warm yellow and the eastern faces slipping into darkness.

Three helicopters were hovering over our former home a few miles away and I could hear more coming.

Cell towers dogged the highway and we had signal.

I brought up Twitter and logged into an account that I never used, @aliensaintrealguy. There was a stream of stupid screed there, dumb stuff like "Moon landing = hoax. Arcturian Alliance = hoax. Superheroes = hoax. Grow up world, they're just trying to control us." Retweets of other conspiracy nuts and tweets about an unhealthy obsession with Nutella.

"What the..." Licia mumbled, looking over my shoulder.

I typed out a new message. "They're coming for me. Now. I have photographic evidence. Proof. They'll be coming for you soon. Run. We'll all burn. Help!"

"Byte," Licia said with a sigh.

I nodded. "One of her bots runs that account, any message that originates elsewhere will set off alarms. She'll figure it out."

I pulled the external battery and the phone died, my eyes going to the helicopters. One was hovering over what I knew to be that eerily smooth sphere of vaporized earth that used to be Casita de Soledad. Two others were slowly spiraling out.

I opened my mouth to apologize to Licia. I had never told her I had a back door to communicate with Byte, just like she had never told me about this cave. I hadn't wanted to worry her. I hadn't wanted to believe I would ever need to use it.

I looked and Licia was staring at me and before I could speak, she gave me a small nod. She had processed all of that already and was moving on.

"They're looking for us," she said.

I nodded.

"What are we going to do?"

I did the chopping hand gesture that means "stop" in American sign language and pointed at my ear. I needed to focus, I needed to hear.

Licia nodded, her eyes scanning the beautiful high desert land laid out before us. This wasn't one of our many sunset walks that we had taken here. This wasn't one of our long, lazy days that made up much of our forced retirement.

This was survival.

I deepened my breath and quieted it, holding it briefly at the end of the inhale and at the end of the exhale. I listened.

I heard the buzz of the highway to the west and of flies nearby. The chirp of bats sending out their ultrasonic radar as they roused themselves for the evening feeding. The scampering of a rabbit, the dried grass moving in the breeze, the distant yip of a coyote. The thump of the distant helicopters and the farther away thump of the approaching helicopters. I heard other vehicles, their engines quiet, their tires crunching over rock.

And I heard voices. Not close, just on the edge of my hearing, so distant that at first I thought I was making it up.

I closed my eyes and continued the slow, deep breaths. The crunch of feet on the ground, the muffled squawk of a walkie-talkie, voices speaking in whispers.

"They're almost here," I signed to Licia.

She nodded and pulled me back into the cool dark of the cave.

7 / BYTE

MY EARS POPPED AS THE PLANE SURGED INTO THE SKY, leaving New York City and the United Stated behind. I peeked out the window and saw the dark blue of the Atlantic below, whitecaps churning in the winds of the approaching nor'easter. I looked back and saw a thin strip of Long Island under a lead-grey sky.

I was in the plush blue seat of first class with mirror shades on and a blue New York Mets baseball cap pulled over my brown hair, dressed in jeans and sweatshirt. I slouched down in my seat and stared out, trying to ignore the fact that Licia wasn't in the seat next to me.

She was working a job for Heroes Incorporated, helping to repair a power plant in Oregon after the earthquake. She had been called out at the last moment, hopping a flight west while I headed east. If you're dealing with high-voltage power what could be better than Lightningirl, the goddess of electricity, who in her former life was a linewoman?

"You'll be okay," she had said when we parted in the Phoenix airport, a swirl of travelers flowing around us, the air dry, barely intelligible announcements coming in over the PA. Her round face was passive, no smile, no frown, no crinkled forehead. She was worried and the statement, while not a question, felt like an aspiration not a reality.

"I will," I had said with as much conviction as I could muster. My stomach felt hollow and I could smell the sharp scent of my own fear.

She held me tight for a long time, told me she loved me, and then I watched her walk down the long hallway that joined two of Sky Harbor's concourses.

The plane jolting pulled me back to reality and I sighed and looked around. First class wasn't full, the seat next to me, Licia's seat, empty. The other passengers were reading books, or tapping on laptops, or reclining and trying to sleep for the long flight to London.

I pushed the panic down and stared at the churning ocean below as the jet surged upward. Soon we were surrounded by grey as we moved into the clouds, more jolts of turbulence rumbling through the hollow tube with fuel-filled wings attached that we rode in.

Air flight is safe, a lot safer than car travel, I get that. I'm a q-morph that can fly, I get that too. But there is something about hurtling through the air at six hundred miles per hour in a heavy machine that can be unsettling.

Well, when you're halfway to a PTSD panic attack it can be. I've been in lots of military aircraft, jumped out of a few helicopters, flown myself into space, but right there, that day, I wanted nothing more than to get out of there and not be stuck for seven hours.

I felt hot and I was starting to sweat. I twisted away from the aisle, took my hat and sunglasses off, shucked my sweatshirt, leaving a plain black T-shirt. But I just felt hotter, my cheeks starting to burn, my breath going shallow. I fiddled with the controls above me, trying to get more air on me, but it wasn't enough.

Another jolt rumbled through the plane and my heart leapt. I looked around, expecting to see other people panicking, but it was just me.

This place was too small. That was it. It wasn't a twelve-by-twelve cell, it was a long hollow tube, but I couldn't get out. I couldn't leave. I couldn't even pace.

On the previous flights on this recruiting tour, I had had Licia with me, chatting, holding my hand, distracting me with news of her parents, talking about the dinner we had just had with my parents.

I hadn't even noticed how small these places were. How trapped I felt. I stared at the grey void of the clouds, hoping it would make me feel less claustrophobic, but it just made it worse. I needed to get out of here. Now. Even if I have to—

"I think you should put your hat and glasses back on, Nik," a voice said, a feminine voice. My heart leapt. Licia was here.

I turned, and a woman was in the seat next to me. She had bright red lips and long black hair, but her eyes were blue and her skin was too light. It wasn't Licia. Dressed in a black turtleneck she had an elegant air to her. I played back what she had said, and yes, there had been an English accent.

Byte.

She put sunglasses on and I spotted a few blond hairs peeking out from underneath what now was clearly a wig. She was in disguise, trying to look like Licia to the very casual viewer.

My heart fell, even though she was the one I was going to London to see. I tried to cover my disappointment by putting my hat and glasses back on.

"How did you..." I began, but trailed off. Asking Byte how she knew I was on this flight was silly. She was a q-morph who could hack the internet with her mind, control any computer with a thought. I'm sure she had a passable ID and a copy of Licia's ticket in her pocket.

She didn't answer me but slipped her soft hand into my sweaty hand and squeezed. "It's going to be all right," she said, her voice calm. Byte was part of Toxicwasteman's League of Villains Extraordinaire (LoVE), but this wasn't like when she tried to seduce me when we first met. This was motherly.

I nodded and took a deep breath letting it out slowly, her rose scent relaxing me just a touch.

"We were hoping this wouldn't happen," she added, her lips turning down into a frown. "But we have a plan."

That "we" meant her and Tom Tyree (aka Toxicwasteman).

I pulled my hand from hers, my cheeks flushed with anger. "It was you that had that last-minute job come up for Licia," I said, suddenly feeling alone again.

"It was necessary," she said. "They really do need her help, we just nudged them a bit."

I looked away back out into the grey, but Byte kept talking.

"I need you to close your eyes, Nik," she said, her voice taking on a quieter, lulling tone. "I need you to remember what you learned in that prison. I need you to deepen your breath, soften your mind. Breathe in and out."

I didn't want to, but I had learned something important there in that prison under Groom Lake. If you can free your mind, there is no prison.

I listened to her lulling voice, smelled her calming rose scent, and remembered what I had learned.

8 / FIGHT OR FLIGHT

MY FEET WERE A MESS, BATTERED BY THE DESERT, PUNCTURED by cactus, and now the rocky floor of the cool cave poking into them. We don't think about our feet all that often, not when they are doing their job, not when things are going well. They're these complex biomechanical collections of bones, joints, ligaments, and muscles that let us run and walk, climb and swim. They are marvels really.

The soldiers were getting closer, the sounds of their boots pounding across the desert, the occasional whispered word clear to me. Licia would be able to hear them soon. She had pulled me to the back of the cave, to the warmth of the uranium hidden in that metal footlocker. She was talking, but I was just staring at our dirty feet.

Casita de Soledad was gone.

Homeland Security and the military were searching for us.

I flew us away from that strange sphere that Project Vulcan had created and yet they had tracked us quickly. They must have had some aerial surveillance in place.

They knew we had survived.

They were going to find us.

I had tweeted, attempted to contact Byte, but I had no idea if she would come through, if she would help me. She had set that account up almost two decades ago. We weren't exactly on friendly terms since things got crazy.

Licia is the practical one, I'm the romantic. She's all business in a crisis, I can often get distracted by the past, or by my worries or by—

"Take it!" Licia hissed, her hand holding a grey rock with gold flecks that was radiating a warmth that I could feel.

After surviving the meteor, what happened at Yellowstone, the damn prison, not to mention the war, here I was with my mind in neutral.

But I was cold, physically cold. We lost our clothes when we transformed earlier and hadn't put any of the clothing on from the footlocker. I grabbed the rock. I took a deep breath. I felt my mind coming back.

Colonel Williams had risked a lot to warn us about Project Vulcan. He wanted us to survive. We all knew the aliens might come back. And then I had gone crazy about the bomb planted below our desert home, about the degree of surveillance we had been under. I had blown it up. I had blown up Casita de Soledad and our lives with it. I had—

"They're almost here. Nik," Licia said, her cool hand on my shoulder. "Snap out of it."

We were out of power. Naked. Cold. All I had was a piece of uranium, its radiation slowly starting to fire me up. Slowly seeping through my hand into my body, reminding me who I was.

"I need a little more time," I said.

She nodded and said, "Don't take too long." She touched my arm with her cool hand. There was no exchange of our energies, no tendrils of yellow and blue-white, we were that tapped out. She grabbed a blanket from the footlocker, wrapped it around herself and walked to the front of the cave.

The blanket was one of those scratchy wool blankets, just like I had in prison. The uranium, while warming, wasn't enough. I had to dig deep like I did the day I got out of that prison.

I grabbed another blanket from the footlocker and put it on the cave floor and sat on it with my legs crossed, my eyes slits. I could see Licia with her blanket wrapped around her, framed by the orange tinged sky of sunset at the mouth of the cave.

I took a deep breath and held the uranium ore to my belly. I let go of everything, like I had learned. I let go of the past and the future, my world nothing more than Licia's silhouette through slitted eyes, my focus soft.

Licia was all that I could see. All my world.

I breathed and my guilt about Casita de Soledad bubbled up and I just noted, thinking "guilt" and letting it go. The traumas of the war, the indignities that I had been subject to, the many times I nearly died, all bubbled up. I noted them. Fear. Regret. Guilt. Worry.

I let it all go.

And I knew that I was just putting those things down, as I breathed in the dry air of the cave, felt the warmth of the uranium grow against my belly. They were not gone, I was still human, I needed to figure it all out. Just like overheavy bags I had been carrying for too long, I set them down. I relaxed.

I heard the soldiers coming close, their boots against the sandy dirt, their breaths quick from exertion. I heard a male voice speaking on a walkie-talkie, saying that we had been found and the high-pitched whine of one of the alien energy weapons charging.

But I didn't care. It felt so good to put all of that baggage down. To breathe. I felt the warmth at my belly, radiating out through my body and I wasn't cold anymore.

"Well, boys," I heard Licia say, her voice distant as if in a dream. "Are you going to just shoot me or are we going to talk first?"

I KNOW I'VE SAID IT BEFORE, BUT IT BEARS REPEATING. Meditation is hard work.

Byte's voice was lulling as the plane vibrated around me. All I could see through my slitted eyes was the back of the seat in front of me. With vipassana meditation, you don't close your eyes all the way, it is more about seeing the true nature of reality, not shutting yourself off from it.

As I breathed, I smelled the rose scent of Byte louder than all the other smells around me. Sweat. Coffee brewing. Alcohol. A random thought came up and I spoke it instead of letting go. "No patchouli today," I whispered to her, my gaze still forward.

She had smelled both of roses and patchouli the day we had met in the LoVE base near the Grand Canyon.

She chuckled softly. "Just breathe, Nik. Let that go, okay? Breathe in the air, feel it rushing in at the back of your nose, feel it filling your body, breathe out the thoughts and the worries."

Noticing it had pleased her, I could tell. And then I was amused at what I was noticing, and then I let that go.

Just the breath coming in, just the breath going out.

And then I could see. Blue tendrils of electricity all around me, running through the shell of the plane, up the back of the chair to the LCD screen.

I kept breathing, but slowly moved my head and saw her. Byte. Humans are a dense tangle of electromagnetic energy with a thick trunk down the spine and a tight blue ball in the skull, but Byte, she was different, or rather, more. The blue tendrils of energy left her head, winding out all over the place in graceful twists and curls. To the LCD monitor in the seatback in front of her, to the phone sitting on the tray table of the passenger across the aisle. A large tendril twisting out of her head and spiking down through the bottom of the plane.

"Good," she said with a smile. She looked so different with the blue lines I could see just below the skin. "You can see now. That's your EMV. Electromagnetic Vision. You must make this second nature."

I smiled, a silly smile, like I was an infant who saw everything as beautiful, like the trace work of blue running through the flight attendant's body as she walked down the aisle. The dense blue splotches of the other passenger's phone, the battery and electronics, with tiny pulses of blue radiating out, the Wi-Fi signal, the phone not in airplane mode.

Ahead, past the passengers whose energy I could see, through the seats, I saw the cockpit and its dense tangle of wires and electricity, its pilot and copilot.

It looked like they were having an intense conversation, their mouths moving rapidly, the copilot flipping switches, which sent out tiny pulses of blue down thin lines. He then looked out the window back towards the wing, and then was talking to the pilot some more.

"There's something wrong," I whispered, trying to hold onto this state, this Electromagnetic Vision.

"What?" she asked.

I slowly turned my head back so I could see the wing with my eyes and with my EMV. We were at elevation, the storm roiling grey below us, blue sky above. The clouds themselves had large blue veins and smaller tendrils flowing through them as electricity churned within the clouds. I could see the outside half of the wing with my eyes and I could see the tracing blue lines of electricity that went to the flaps, that wound around the engine.

There, in the middle engine, I saw the blue flicker, a sparking, and the blue winding around the engine winked out and all that was left was a blue blotch that scuttled along towards the back of the engine. The relentless white noise of the engines lessoned and I felt the plane slow, twisting slightly.

I stood, Byte was asking me what was going on, but I ignored her and moved into the aisle, with my EMV gaze looking at the opposite wing, which still had energy pulsing through it.

"This is not good," I whispered, glancing back at Byte. The blue tendrils coming from her head were stronger, pulsing brightly, more of them reaching out, connecting with every piece of electronics in the plane.

I felt the plane execute a slow turn, heading us back towards the west.

"Excuse me, sir," the flight attendant said when I got to the front of the plane, "you'll have to go sit down." She was all pulsing blue lines, my EMV making it hard to see what she really looked like. But I could still tell there was worry there written on her face.

I removed my hat and glasses and her eyes widened.

"We have a problem here," I said evenly. "I need to talk to the captain."

The blue bundle that was her brain sparked brighter at the front of her head.

"There's something out there," Byte whispered in my ear, so low that I doubted anyone else could hear it. "It disabled one engine and... it's moving towards the next."

Something out there? Was she talking about the scuttling blue blotch I saw? What the hell could it be?

I turned to her and saw that the blue lines and tendrils leaving her head were denser and brighter than everyone else's. She was a quantum biomorph, her form changed permanently on that day in 2003 when the cosmic rays hit. As I looked at her it became clear that controlling electronics with her mind was only the beginning of what happened to her. Her whole brain had changed. Her whole nervous system.

"Can you do something about it?" I asked

She shrugged and in my meditative, childlike state I found the firing of the nerves that sparked right as the muscles in her shoulders moved to be fascinating. "It's... I don't know what it is. It's not... normal. I don't know."

"Sir, you'll have to sit down," the flight attendant was saying, I think she might have said it multiple times, but she was keeping her distance from me, so I suspect she knew who I was.

I held up my index finger and in my calm state was able to spark the tip neutrino yellow for just a second, a very limited transformation, so there was no doubt.

"How far out are we?" I asked as the flight attendant gawked.

"Ninety minutes from JFK," Byte answered from behind, a strain in her voice. "This thing... whatever did this... It's at the second engine now. It's... I'm almost there."

The hum of the second engine died and I almost stumbled as the plane noticeably slowed. There were murmurs from the cabin behind us.

"Too late," Byte said.

We were ninety minutes out, a storm over the Atlantic below us, and no engines.

"How long can we glide?" I asked Byte.

She paused, her head tilted like she was trying to retrieve a distant memory. "Twenty minutes... tops."

The pulsing blue lines of electromagnetic energy faded as I

almost slipped out of my meditative state, almost lost my EMV. But I took a deep breath, noting the worry and letting it go.

"I think you better let me speak to the captain, now," I said to the flight attendant with the best smile I could offer.

"He's coming," Byte whispered, again so low that I doubt anyone else could hear it, but the fear in her voice clear. "But he won't be in time."

I knew she wasn't talking about the captain but about Toxi-cwasteman. Whatever was to be done, we had to do it.

10 / CAPTURE

THE DESERT HAS ALWAYS FELT LIKE MY HOME. I WAS BORN IN Phoenix and kicked around Arizona all my life until Licia and I ended up in the central Arizona desert for our exile at Casita de Soledad. The desert doesn't hide its dangers. It's full of spiny plants and fanged reptiles, dry air and relentless heat. You know exactly what you are getting from the desert. It's hard, but it's obvious.

But people... they are not like that, not at all. Not when it comes to groups when the dynamics of politics and bureaucracy creep in. They're nothing like the desert, their poison and danger largely hidden.

Like Homeland Security planting a bomb under our little piece of desert. Planting explosives to take out the high-tension power lines that could make Licia into Lightningirl. Having so much surveillance on us that even when our home and everything around it was vaporized they tracked us with ease.

Homeland is not like the rattlesnake whose tail warns you, whose fangs make it clear just what kind of danger you are in.

Homeland hides behind paperwork and "need to know" and layers of bureaucracy and security.

And they are not like Toxicwasteman whose hunger and danger were written all over his sickly green quantum form. With him, you knew it could go bad at any moment, get weird, you could rest assured he would do something unusual.

These thoughts were gnats as I meditated, as my EMV came to life, as I saw that there were four soldiers confronting Licia, as I heard the thump-thump of a helicopter closing in on our location.

They shot orange energy balls at Licia, they lit up the cave with garish light but I just closed my eyes.

They shot purple energy balls into the cave, seeking me, and in my flesh and blood form they did nothing to me, nothing to the uranium I held. I wasn't Neutrinoman, I was just Nik, thirsty, hungry, and naked in the middle of a small cave with beat up feet.

I took a deep breath, the scratchy wool blanket beneath me, the piece of uranium ore pressed to my belly, the warmth of it growing, making me feel safe when nothing should have made me feel safe right then.

The soldiers were in the cave now. Licia had talked to them, tried to stall them, but all their words had just slipped by me. The soldiers were talking to me, shouting words, fear clear in their voice, clear in their scent. Even with my slitted eyes I could see the blue tracery of their bodies, the tangled ball of their brains, the strong trunk of their spinal cords.

Three of them stood pointing their weapons at me. One of them fired purple energy balls into me repeatedly. The balls, I was curious to note, looked the same to my eyes as they did to my electromagnetic vision: coruscating, spiking balls of energy about the size of a fist.

I didn't think, but took another deep breath and pressed the uranium ore to my belly. It was hidden underneath my hands, they couldn't know it was there. I exhaled and I pressed harder. It didn't hurt, it felt good, it felt right.

And then their rough hands grabbed me, their scared voices tinged with fear. They pulled my hands behind my back to handcuff me, but the ore was gone. I wasn't quite sure how I did it, but it was in me. It was part of me and I felt warm... so warm.

11 / ANOTHER PLAN

IT ALL TOOK TOO LONG. SECONDS TICKING PAST FELT LIKE hours. This metal tube with fuel-filled wings attached was falling. Well, not falling, yet, not quite that. Without the engines it was slowing, the wings providing less lift, and we were gliding down to the storm clouds and the chaotic ocean below with over three hundred people on board.

The rumbling of the engines was long gone, the relative silence eerie. My EMV was still with me and I could see back to both engines, lifeless, no electricity running through them except for the odd blue blotch in one. I could see that the flaps were still operational.

The flight attendant had gotten on the phone and talked to the captain, but he wouldn't see me. She left and went back to deal with the scared passengers, their voices having become fearful.

Byte went after her, argued with her, and then gave up and came back and she was looking at me, still dressed in her black wig, her sunglasses still on. Even now with the future so uncertain, she wanted to retain her anonymity.

She had said, "He's coming, but he won't be in time." She had meant Tom Tyree, Toxicwasteman. He was flying towards us to... Not to rescue me, I didn't need rescuing, and surely not for the three hundred souls on board. He was coming for Byte. And that... it helped me somehow. He cared about her enough to risk himself. He "loved" her—whatever love meant to a sociopath like him.

"What can I do?" I asked, guilt lying on me heavily. I'm no Superman with powers that can be applied benignly. I'm a controlled nuclear reaction, my touch just as damaging as Toxicwasteman's. I could survive this. I didn't know about any of the others.

My EMV was fading and I could see her face clearer, her brow furrowed in concentration, several blue tendrils that headed into the cockpit getting more active, sparking blue lights zipping back and forth. She was doing... well, I didn't know what, but it seemed to relate to my questions.

And then her brow relaxed. "Be the engine," she said.

I smiled. Not because I was happy, but because I was relieved. I could do something besides go down with the plane.

I looked around, the hatch was there, but that would depressurize the cabin and slow the plane down. How to get out?

The flight crew would know, but that captain had refused to talk to me, the flight attendants were busy. There had to be a way.

My gaze wandered, my EMV fading in the worry, but not gone. I glanced down, there were blue lines of energy running down there. Of course. I was in a tube, the top half of a tube. If I could get into the lower half, the cargo hold, I could cut my way out without depressurizing the cabin. And then, somehow, I would have to be the engine.

Byte had beat me to it. She was on the floor of the mess opening a trapdoor, a strange look on her face. I would call it sheepish, but that's not quite right. It was a shy look as if she was asking a lot of me, but also as if she wasn't sure hope was even called for.

My stomach tightened and the EMV left.

"I can do this," I said as I crouched down beside her, wishing I could see the eyes behind her sunglasses.

She nodded, her cool hands pressing something into my ear. "If you can, keep from melting it," she began, "then I can talk to you." And then her lips didn't move, but I heard her in my ear, "To get this plane down safely, we'll have to communicate."

I nodded and pressed my finger to the metal she had inserted. It was cool and hard. The same kind of thing Toxicwasteman had in his ear when I saw him right after the Hoover Dam was destroyed.

"This is a fly by wire plane," she said in my ear, a smile on her red lips. "If they won't cooperate, I'll be taking it over."

I nodded, but hesitated for a moment. The pitch of the voices from the passenger section was getting strident and the sensation of the plane falling was getting more pronounced.

"Take care of yourself," I said.

She nodded. I climbed down the short ladder and she closed the hatch above me.

I THOUGHT WE WERE OVER THIS. BEING DRAGGED AROUND naked with scratchy wool blankets hastily thrown over us. Only the tiniest of gestures towards retaining our dignity that the military could manage.

The cloudless western horizon was tinged with orange, the kind of restrained sunset Licia and I had watched almost every night up here. The rolling desert was slipping into darkness, the yip of a coyote barely discernable over the shouts of soldiers and the thump-thump of the approaching helicopter.

Licia's black hair, rumpled and staticky, reminded me of what it looks like when she is Lightningirl. Her brown eyes caught mine and I gave her a small smile, hoping to reassure her. Her brow furrowed and she shook her head a tiny bit. We were just outside the cave surrounded by four soldiers, three with rifles pointed at us, one with an alien energy weapon strapped to his back, the silver tube pointing at me.

My EMV was still strong, the blue trace work of their nervous systems clear. Licia's, though, was different. It was much stronger, a deeper blue, with blue-white pulses zooming back and forth. And this is when she's completely tapped of energy.

We had learned, we had believed, that quantum metamorphs, like Licia and I, were normal flesh and blood before we transformed. And that quantum biomorphs, like Chaosboy and Byte, were transformed once, with Quin Rask being the exception and a little bit of both. Seeing Licia like this reminded me that it was just not that simple.

We had all changed permanently and some of us could transform into other forms.

"Gentlemen," I began. "I would appreciate it if you, at least, pointed your rifles down and let me have a moment with my wife."

I haven't described the soldiers yet, I haven't told you that two of them were white men, the third an older man of Latin heritage, and the fourth a woman. That they were dressed in fatigues, wore helmets, had gear strapped to their waists and tall boots on. That one had a deep gruff voice, another one a boyishly high voice, the woman hardly talking.

And they did have a lot of gear and they might have been as I just mentioned, but I don't remember. My EMV was strong, making ethnicity difficult to see. My mind was in a meditative state where I saw things more broadly and couldn't tell you if one of them had a mustache or if the woman's hair was braided.

But more than that, they were stand-ins for the forces that had kept us here for so long, kept us small. So even in my meditative state, I didn't want to know them.

This wasn't like it was back in the prison, where it was paramount to know something about one of my guards. That his name was Evan and he liked football not soccer, had lost a girl when he served in Iraq. Evan Saunders who had died saving my life. I needed to humanize the people around me then because I was starved of contact. Now, below the peaceful Zen state was that baggage that I had put down—the anger for what they had done and the shame for how I had handled it. The grief for what we had just lost.

I was desperate, surrounded by soldiers in the desert, our home just destroyed, my only hope a piece of uranium ore I had managed to somehow take into my body. My clearly never-quite-human body. The rock was whole and sitting just below the skin or in my stomach, or maybe my body absorbed the ore, so desperate it was for energy, pieces of it all through my body. I didn't know. I didn't think about it then. I just wanted escape.

They were talking to me now, these soldiers I didn't want to know, who were just following their orders. They were shouting, pointing their weapons at me, but still I walked to Licia. My hands were cuffed behind me, so I couldn't hold her, but I pressed myself against her. I smiled as I felt my body feeding hers, the old energy dance coming back.

She sucked in a breath, she hadn't expected it, and I whispered, "This will have to be fast."

I felt her head nod against my chest.

I didn't tell her it would be dangerous—she knew that.

I was about to do it, trigger the change, when I heard them. A low buzz rising above the gentle whisper of the breeze, barely perceptible against the thump-thump of the helicopter that was almost here.

I looked up and saw them. Drones. Quadcopter drones. Hundreds of them flying over the desert like a swarm of locust.

Byte. She got my message. Boy did she get my message.

INTERLUDE 1

"You gotta stop this," Licia said, her voice surprising me as I typed away on the laptop computer. Adrenaline dumped into my blood-stream, and I jumped and cursed.

"Stop what?" I asked, keeping my voice as calm as I could. I can't tell you where we were, but for the sake of the story let's say it was in a bland hotel room in shades of brown and off-white with an overloud air conditioner pumping dry cold air into the room to beat back the heat.

"This." She pointed at the screen where I was lamenting the loss of Casita de Soledad and all we had built. Feeling bad about my PTSD and lack of control.

Things were tense between us. We were in hiding (sort of, you'll get a glimpse of it soon) and we were still being hunted. I didn't speak, I just stared at her.

She sighed and bounced down onto the edge of the bed and held out her hand, a kind look on her round face. I took her hand and our bodies did their reassuring exchange of energy.

"Look, Nik," she began. "I know you feel bad about it. I know you need to write to get it out. It's just..." She trailed off, biting her lip.

"What?"

"Don't bore your reader. They get you feel bad. You don't need to bring it up over and over, even though that's what's going on in your head."

I blinked and wanted to jerk my hand out of hers, but I didn't. It was connection with my beloved and I needed that.

She smiled again, it was strained and tight, but filled with empathy. "I miss our home, too. I miss what we built and I miss the ease of those days, but..." She looked around the small room as if there was a magnificent landscape to see. "Look at what we are doing now," she said, her voice hushed. "It was hell getting here, but... This is better. You know it is."

I nodded slowly, my mind still in the past.

"You are certainly not bored anymore," she added.

I smiled in spite of myself. Boredom is not good for me, and this current adventure is certainly not boring.

"And thanks to Project Vulcan, your story got a hell of a lot better." She read my puzzled look and continued. "You started out writing about the past from a safe, secure position. The 'Interludes' of yours were minor, just a taste of our current lives. Well... now, both the past and the present are pretty amazing stories."

She stopped with a smile and the humming of the air conditioner seemed overloud.

"I still feel bad," I said quietly.

She nodded slowly. "I know. I do too. But for your reader, just get on with the story. They know you feel bad."

And Licia was right. What she was saying was in no way comfortable, but it was entirely true. So enough lamenting a single mistake. On with the story.

13 / DEPLANING

LIGHTS FLICKERED ON AS I DROPPED DOWN INTO THE 787's cargo hold, long strips of LEDs running along the low ceiling. I didn't know if they were motion controlled or Byte had turned them on for me, but I was glad I could see.

Not that there was much to see. I was stooped over and couldn't stand. This being the lower portion of the tube, the floor wasn't that wide. There was a diagonal section of wall that joined the horizontal floor to the vertical wall. This was because of the tube, trying to create a squarish space in a round object. Towards the back of the plane, I could see shipping containers that fit snugly into this space with only an inch or two between them. The floor was metal with regular divots that were used to anchor the cargo containers.

In front of me was a wall with a small door that led into an area under the cockpit. I assumed that had equipment in it.

For a moment, a thin second, I looked around with wonder at the scratched and well-used metal surfaces. At the door and the strange things that must lie beyond. At the shipping containers with luggage and who knows what else in it. I was the guy who took a janitorial job just so I could see the inside of a nuclear power plant. I wanted nothing more than to explore.

But there was no time.

Earlier, I mentioned fuel-filled wings, but I had no idea where else they might store fuel. Fitting something reasonably rectangular inside a tube meant there was space underneath the floor and past the walls. Would they store fuel there? This plane had to have enough to cross the Atlantic.

There was not time to debate or explore. I chose the diagonal section reasoning that since it was like that to accommodate the tube, there wouldn't be anything beyond it.

I crouched down, transformed my right arm, held my breath and punched through it.

There was no explosion, but the air in the small space whooshed out, sucking my breath away with it. Outside the hole was undifferentiated grey—we were flying in the storm clouds now.

"Hurry up," Byte said in my ear. "We've dropped into the storm."

"I'm working on it," I shouted against the roar of the wind.

"Go faster."

I transformed, slowly, keeping my reaction low, trying to not do too much damage in here, not wanting to melt the earpiece.

I widened the hole and marveled at just how thin this metal tube was that hurled through the air. There were ribs circling the tube and several layers of thin metal, but it wasn't much.

I shoved my head through the hole into the thick grey and saw the dead engine hanging lifeless on the port wing.

Now what?

To be the engine, as Byte had suggested, I had to get to the engine.

"I'm going out," I said, having no idea what I was going to do.

"Good luck," the reply quickly came back, her voice steady and emotionless as it had been before through the earbud. She wasn't actually talking, she was using her powers to transmit her voice to the earbud. It was kind of like a computerized version of her voice and right then it spooked me.

"What is your name?" I shouted, not sure how she could hear me with wind out here.

"Excuse me?" she asked, again no emotion.

I couldn't give her a long speech about how humanizing those who appeared to be my enemy had helped me survive prison. How I hated that LoVE had turned "Toxicwasteman" into "Toxic" and "Chaosboy" into "Chaos," seeming to discard their humanity with it. I couldn't tell her that before I thrust myself into the unknown, to attempt something that might not work, that she might not survive, that I wanted to know her name. That I needed to at least know someone's name on the plane.

"Please! Tell me your name." I shouted instead, shoving myself through the hole and falling into the grey.

14 / ESCAPE

SUMMER 2025, CENTRAL ARIZONA

THE DRONES WERE BUZZING ALL OVER THE DESERT, BUT THE bulk of them were coming towards us. A group swarmed the nearly-here helicopter, a UH1-D with the side door open and two soldiers with alien energy weapons pointed towards us.

At least a dozen descended on us, their cameras swiveling, catching the details of our capture, of our hastily covered nudity and our handcuffed hands.

"Hold still," I whispered, still pressed to Licia, feeling my body feeding her energy, seeing the tendrils of yellow pass from me to her and feeling the barest zaps of electrical energy coming back from her.

I thought of the drones as bats, not to be feared, knowing that they could fly with great agility, knowing Byte was behind them.

But the soldiers didn't react as well. They shouted. They started firing at them, but I just ignored it, breathing deeply, feeling the energy exchange, seeing my EMV deepen as I saw the darkening desert with new eyes. I could see the blue tracery of a rabbit sprinting away from us, spooked by the gunfire. The drones looking like some kind of blue fairies flying and bobbing in the air. Back towards Casita de Soledad I could see a few large blobs of blue, helicopters I presumed, being harassed by more sprightly pricks of blue, the drones.

Byte was getting the footage of what had happened. The military had clearly violated the Quantum Metamorph Accord of 2020 with Project Vulcan.

As the three soldiers fired, as the fourth one still kept the alien energy weapon trained on us, my smooth mind snagged on a thought, my EMV fled and I cursed.

"What?" Licia whispered.

"The drones. They got here so fast," I said.

"Oh..." She got it. Those drones getting here this quickly meant that the military had not been the only ones watching us closely. Byte had been too. She somehow got these drones in position with solar cells to keep them charged, hidden so that we didn't find them in our wanderings and neither did the military.

"Later," Licia whispered. She knew where my head was going, could feel the shiver pass through my body. I was no longer feeling so warm with that uranium ore inside me. "We should just go."

I nodded, but the Zen state was gone.

Around us the rifles fired, the drones buzzed, some falling to the bullets, and the helicopter fled like a hawk chased away by a group of sparrows.

"He can't get us both," Licia whispered. She was referring to the soldier with the alien energy weapon. It shot either purple or orange energy balls, designed to strip either me or Licia of our powers. It took a bit of time to switch.

And my best guess was they had it tuned to me, but that was a mistake. I couldn't stun them or do much without risking their lives, but Lightningirl could.

I took a deep breath, more drones falling around us, the helicopter getting farther away, my EMV returning.

I flipped the switch, transforming quickly, the handcuffs

sparking against the yellow of my neutrino form, the metal starting to glow. The wool blanket started burning, bits of it falling to the sandy soil below me.

I turned quickly and extended my hand in a defensive gesture, the yellow column shooting out of my chest, forming a shield in front of us.

He saw it all, of course, the soldier whose face I don't remember, the one with the alien energy weapon. He fired, purple energy balls as predicted, and I could feel them as they crashed into my shield, tapped my energy, but the shield held.

Behind me I could feel a sharp tingling as Licia found her q-morph form. At the same time, the other three soldiers ignored the drones and started firing on us.

It didn't matter, though. Neutrinoman and Lightningirl have always been better together than apart.

The drones buzzed, the bullets bounced off the shield, the orange energy balls slammed into it with a sizzle, the shield flickering, but holding.

I was well powered, that uranium ore giving me energy to spare. But when Lightningirl was fully transformed it was all over.

She stepped beside me, a blue-white coruscating electrical reaction in the form of a beautiful woman. She extended both hands, small tendrils of energy leaping from the four soldiers to her fingers. She wasn't zapping them with power, she was drawing energy from them. Just like she had first done in Yellowstone when we faced the stampede of Buffalo.

Soon the four soldiers were on the ground snoring.

"What now?" she asked.

And that was a good question. What now? It felt good to be Neutrinoman and Lightningirl again, but Casita de Soledad was still destroyed, Homeland Security would still be hunting us, and we still had an interview to get to.

A single drone hovered in front of us and I smiled and nodded at it, thanking Byte for her help.

"Anymore secret caches I don't know about?" I asked.

"Well..." she said with a sheepish grin on her electrical face.

I laughed. I loved my practical preparing wife more than ever. I took her into my arms and flew us away.

FALL 2006, OVER THE ATLANTIC OCEAN

I FELL, FIRST THE LONG TAPERING WING OF THE BOEING 787 passing within inches of me. I almost crashed into that fuel-filled wing with a dead engine attached. Then, the dark grey of the dense clouds took me, and I couldn't see the plane. Winds buffeting me and sections of the clouds lit brightly as lightning discharged.

"Shit!" I swore, jetting back to where I thought the plane should be, but it wasn't there. It was all grey, all clouds, nothing but the intermittent flashes to differentiate it.

What could I do? Fly below the clouds and wait for the plane to come out? By then it would have slowed more, making saving it much harder.

Not knowing what else to do, I tilted myself down.

"Your fifty... meters above," a bland voice crackled in my ear. "And... meters behind us."

Byte. She had access to the plane, access to their radar, could somehow see me. But the earbud, it wasn't working well. Was I melting it?

I flew faster, losing some elevation and tried to lessen the reaction around my left ear.

"Where are..." I began, just as the plane emerged out of the grey in front of me. "I see you... commencing with operation 'Be the Engine.'" I was trying to be flip, make light of it, but I was worried.

I had to push the plane to be the engine. I had to do that in a way that didn't directly threaten the passengers or the integrity of the plane, so that ruled out the fuselage. I couldn't use the wings, because, you know, fuel filled. That left the engine.

"I have done everything I can to shut off the fuel supply to both engines," Byte said in my ear, the static gone.

So the engine it was.

A jet engine is a big fan in front, a nozzle that expels hot gas in the back and a compressor, combustor, and turbine in between.

The combustor was my worry. If I melted my way to it, exposed the fuel line... well, that would be bad. This plane was fueled for a flight all the way across the Atlantic that we had barely started.

This also required some difficult modulation of my form. I had to tamp down the reaction where I met the engine but produce as much thrust as possible. So that means, you guessed it, time for the butt thruster.

I flew behind the engine and found that the exhaust cone, that round pointy bit at the back of the engine, was still rotating. Air was still flowing through the system, making it turn. I had been planning on melting the point off and pushing there, but how would that work if it was spinning? If I was off axis even a little bit, the thrust would be inconsistent.

The back edge of the engine cowling had a scalloped tooth pattern around and I saw there was space between the main part of the engine and the cowling where the front fan blew the air that didn't go through the main engine.

It was all I had.

I slammed myself into that gap, my reaction a little hot still, my arms by my side, burying myself in there.

There wasn't much to see, the dark inside of cowling on one side, and the exterior of the jet engine assembly on the other, with some struts joining the two. All of this illuminated by the flickering yellow of my reaction. I couldn't see anything up ahead. The sounds of the wind were strangely muffled and echoing in here.

"Here goes," I said, pulling my legs up and wedging myself in tighter and letting the butt thruster rip.

This was all Byte, and the flight crew if they had wised up, now. They had to use what thrust I could give them to get the plane closer to land.

"That's helping, Nik," Byte said in my ear. "But that's not enough. We need more... a lot more."

I nodded, although no one could see me, and steeled for the effort when in the dim light, I was confronted by a... I'm not sure what it was. A robot, I guess, but not like any I had seen before.

It was a silver-skinned, six-legged construct that moved with a fluidity I've never seen in a machine before. It glowed, filling the area with thin silver light that fought with my flicking yellow. Its body was about twelve inches across and it had something of a head jutting forth with a single rounded eye. It scuttled up to me, its head tilting this way and that, looking nothing less than curious. Its eye was reflective and I could see myself and the thrust shooting out my butt in it.

"Umm... I think I found what disabled the engine."

"What is it?" Byte asked in my ear.

"A... ahhh. A robot, I guess, but not like any robot I've ever seen."

This is what had done it, disabled the engine, I knew that, but it was... I don't know. Cute.

"What do you want?" I asked it.

It scuttled forward, another arm growing out of where its little neck was, on the end of this was a small pincher.

I saw my quizzical expression in its eye and then it danced

close, the pincher jabbing me and then it danced back, a sparking yellow bit of my neutrino form in the pincher.

What the hell?

It held it up to its eye examining it closely.

"It took a sample of me," I shouted. "It's examining me."

"This is not good," Byte's calm voice said in my ear. "It's sending out a strong signal. It's transmitting data."

THE SMELL OF COFFEE SLOWLY ENTICED ME BACK TO consciousness, but I resisted, pulling the blankets tighter around me, burying my head in the pillow, reveling in the soft comfort of the flannel sheets.

I listened for Licia, but she wasn't in bed with me, she must be up, that's who started the coffee. I wondered what we would do today, work on the new greenhouse, undoubtedly. We were still amending the soil and planting. I loved to watch Licia around the plants, how she would suck the life out the weeds, traces of electricity jumping to her outstretched fingers, and she would do the opposite to the plants she wanted to grow, feeding them trickles of energy that they would use to burst forth with fruit.

I turned over on my stomach, rubbing my face against the flannel sheets. They were musty, as if they had been in a closet for a long time. I could hear Licia's feet tapping on a wooden floor, it sounded like she was pacing.

Wait... flannel? It's too hot at Casita de Soledad for flannel. And we don't have wood floors.

And then it all descended on me. My mania on discovering Project Vulcan and the extent Homeland had been surveilling us. How badly I had handled it, setting the bomb off and vaporizing our home, destroying all that we had built together. The march through the desert to Licia's secret cache. The uranium ore. Contacting Byte via a fake Twitter account. The drones coming and our escape.

I groaned and sat up, my head thick, and looked around. Flannel sheets meant Flagstaff and there were pine trees out the little window, but the cabin was small and rustic and all I could see out the window were towering pine trees, all I could hear were birds.

It all came back to me.

After our escape, as the darkness descended on Arizona, I had flown us fast and low north up onto the Mogollon Rim, skirting Flagstaff and the San Francisco Peaks, over the lower expanses of desert that sat between Flagstaff and the Grand Canyon, and then into the Grand Canyon, zooming above the Colorado River, zipping through salmon-colored limestone canyons in the dying light, up long side canyons past the cream-colored Kaibab limestone into the ponderosa pine forest of the North Rim.

We flew fast, Licia shouting me directions the whole way, riding on my back and holding my neck so tight if I had been flesh, she would have choked me.

She hates flying and really hates riding on my back, but this was not a gentle jaunt into orbit. I was flying as low as I dared, well below radar, in the dim evening light, staying away from populated areas as much as possible. I had to go fast. I had to be maneuverable.

We flew until we found this isolated and rustic cabin where Licia gratefully hopped off my back, let go of her q-morph form, pulled a key from under a rock, and let us in.

"My cousin's," she said by way of explanation.

We talked, for a long time, our words carrying us around in

circles, and then she cried, and I cried, and we went to bed and held each other until sleep finally came.

This life had brought us much to grieve. I had hoped we were past losing this much, past this kind of grief, seeing all we had created destroyed, but we were not.

I moved slowly, my body feeling like it might break easily, like delicate stemware in rough hands. This wasn't because of yesterday's tangle with Project Vulcan, and my body was still fully charged from the uranium ore. This was my emotional state impinging on my physical state.

There was a ratty blue robe on the end of the bed and some slippers. I put them on and stumbled out of the bedroom.

Licia stopped her pacing and looked at me, but didn't look long, her eyes only flicking over me before she tightened the tie on her faded red robe and continuing her pacing.

The cabin was old, the wood paneled walls showing the patina of time, the tongue-and-groove floor scratched and scarred. There was a kitchenette on one wall, a couch, an old rocking chair, and that was it.

It was a bit cold, so I went over to the small iron woodstove that sat in the corner opposite the kitchenette, opened the squeaky door, and stacked some pieces of wood in.

"I'm so sorry," I said, my eyes locked on the wood. Her pacing stopped for just a moment and then resumed.

The words seemed hollow. I wanted to elaborate in a way that defended me, something like, "I'm sorry I have PTSD from all we've been through and can't stand the thought of being watched 24/7." But that wasn't an apology and I gulped it down like a pill nearly too large to swallow.

I wanted her to rage, to be mad, to throw things at me. She was the practical one, she kept her head all during yesterday's madness when I nearly lost mine. But today, I knew she would be feeling it. The adrenaline was gone... and so was our lives as we knew it.

I stuck my index finger out, held it near the wood, and shot out some neutrino thrust, just like I shot from my hands and feet (and sometimes by butt) when I fly. Yesterday's madness had helped me remember some of my long unused abilities. The wood quickly caught fire and the crackling noise was some small bit of comfort. It was summer and would be warm outside today, but any comfort seemed in order.

"The interview is when?" I asked, watching the yellow fire dance hungrily over the dry wood. I knew when it was, I just needed to hear her talk.

"Want some coffee?" she asked, as her socked feet continued their back and forth trajectory.

I nodded and walked over to the kitchenette, timing it so I didn't interfere with her pacing. The counters had dust on them, the cabin not seeing much use. We were at the end of a rutted dirt road way off the grid. The solar panels didn't work anymore, but Licia had charged the batteries last night, which apparently worked well enough to power a coffeemaker.

I poured coffee into the mug sitting there by the coffeemaker and promptly burned my mouth, but I didn't care.

The interview was still a week away. Could we stay here the whole time? How long would it take the military and Homeland Security to find us?

"They know we headed north," I mumbled, half to myself.

"And it's not like there won't be reports of Neutrinoman sightings," Licia added. There were numerous websites setup that tracked us, and this sighting will be an unusual one.

We had used the Grand Canyon like someone evading a tracker would have used a river. We immersed ourselves into it, trying to throw off our pursuers. We had made sure we were seen heading both upstream into Utah and downstream farther into Arizona.

"I'm sorry," I said again. I was standing in front of the crackling fire hoping its primal pleasure would help.

Licia stopped pacing and her eyes finally met mine and what I saw there made my stomach tumble. She wasn't sad and she was far past mad. She was furious.

"For what?" she asked, cocking her head.

She knew for what, but wanted to hear me say it. Why did she want to hear me say it?

I swallowed hard. "For destroying our home. For..." I wanted to say more, but couldn't. The shame and the guilt felt like they were smothering me, this great weight on my chest that made it hard to breath.

Her hands balled into fists and tears formed in her eyes. Furious yes, but there were other powerful emotions at play.

"Don't apologize," she said, her right foot creeping forward as if the need to pace was irresistible.

"If... I... Maybe..." I sucked in a breath. I didn't want the tears of last night to come back. I didn't have the strength.

Licia chewed on her lip, staring at me, her hands still fists at her side. "Don't apologize," she said, but quieter this time. "I can't..." She looked away, shaking her head. "Just don't apologize."

I nodded, feeling sick to my stomach, my mind screaming at me that I had destroyed not only our home, but also our marriage. That my weakness, my inability to let it be, had just cost me what I valued most in this world. Licia.

I put the coffee down on the windowsill. "I'm... I'm going to go for a walk," I said.

"That's a good idea," she replied.

I couldn't look at her, I stumbled outside in a worn robe and slippers into the forest.

"WE NEED MORE THRUST," BYTE SAID IN MY EAR, THE computerized version of her voice much too calm and kind of freaking me out. "We need it now."

I was wedged between the main jet assembly and the exterior surface of the 787's jet engine, a support strut against my shoulder, trying to replace the thrust of two dead engines. I also had an unwanted companion.

The glowing silver alien robot danced forward, its pincher jabbing my head, taking another sample of me. A larger one, the size of a pea, yellow motes of a piece of my neutrino form dancing in its pincher, somehow not melting them, its single bulbous eye staring at the sample and then at me, the strain on my face reflected in its eye.

"Can't you do something about this thing!" I shouted.

I needed to focus, but couldn't with this alien construct taking samples of me, transmitting data out, undoubtedly about what it was learning.

The alien Sarah had said the hostilities would end while she "spoke," while the council debated the fate of the Earth. Then why had this little beast disabled the plane and started taking samples of me?

"I can feel it," Byte said in my ear. "I can see its transmission, but I can't quite break through. It's different. It's still transmitting... a lot of data."

And then it dawned on me. The two were linked. It disabled the plane *so* it could take samples of me.

Maybe the council had finished. Maybe our fate had been decided and this was preparation for their final assault.

I shook my head. I didn't have time for this. I ignored the robot for a moment and focused on heating up my internal nuclear reaction to produce more thrust, but then the sample the robot held winked out into nothingness and it danced forward towards me, the small pads on the end of its feet somehow holding fast to the metal against torrent of wind passing through.

"No!" I shouted, and much to my surprise a yellow shield sprang forth from my forehead and shoved the robot back. That shield had always come out of my chest, it had always happened when my hands were thrust forth in a defensive gesture, not when I was thrusting as hard as I could with my hands pinned to my side, and not from my head.

The robot landed on its back, its six legs flailing in the air, but it didn't last long. Without its padded silver feet keeping it anchored to the metal, the wind picked it up and threw it at me, some silver, alien, robot, spider thing.

I reacted again, my mind wanting to lash out and my neutrino form following. The shield dropped, and a sharp beam of yellow jabbed forth, stabbing the robot in its center, running clean through it, the hole glowing orange around the edge. The construct went limp and bounced off my neutrino form on the way out.

"I got it!"

I smiled, but only for a moment.

That thing that I had just done, that neutrino laser was brand new, and it was just like a laser. It passed right through the robot and jabbed into a tube running to the interior assembly of the engine and fuel started spewing forth, mixing with the air and combusting when it hit me.

"That's a little better..." Byte's calm voice began. "Oh. We're losing fuel out of the port wing."

Yeah. No kidding. I couldn't see anything through the flames, and while this was apparently adding a little to the thrust, I worried about the additional heat this was producing. How long could the engine hold up?

"I can't shut it off," she said, "the leak is past any valving I control. I can pump some of the fuel out, but that will unbalance the plane. Do you know what's going on?"

Again, her voice was too damn calm. My face was full of flames. I needed to think.

"No. Wait." I shouted, my mouth opening and filling with flames. Not that it mattered. I wasn't human. I had an air cavity in my neutrino form, but I didn't need to breathe. I used it to pull air in so I could speak, so I could feel normal.

Something tickled in my brain. Shields popping out of my head. Yellow lasers shooting forth. These were new things that I could do. There must be more new things. Byte's words "Be the engine" mixed in and...

"Neutrino, it's me, Toxic." Tom Tyree's voice was a surprise, and chased off my coalescing thoughts, like a kid running at a flock of seagulls on the beach. "I asked Byte to patch me through."

It was too much. Dampening the reaction of my upper body so I don't just melt through the engine, thrusting harder than I ever had before, dealing with an alien robot, and now Toxicwasteman wanted to have a little chat?

"Listen, brother," he continued. "I need you to find a way. I need you to save Gayle. You asked her what her name is. It's Gayle and..." His voice nearly broke. Unlike Byte, this was really his voice, he must have one of the earbuds like I do and has been talking to Byte—no, Gayle—as he flies toward us.

"Look, I'll do anything you want, anything you ask, just find a way to save her and I'll..." He trailed off.

"I'm trying!" I shouted, pushing harder, engulfed in flames, knowing there was no way I could do this for over an hour and get us back.

The flames. There was something about the fuel and the flames, how the jet fuel mixed with the torrent of air before hitting me and burning. If I could just get my mind to work.

"I know you are," he said, "but I need you to reach deeper. I need you to find more. Not for me, but for Gayle."

But it was for him, I could hear it in his voice. He needed Gayle. The sociopathic villain Tom Tyree needed someone. I didn't understand it, but I dug deeper. I thrust harder.

"That's a little better," Byte's computerized voice said, "but we will still come down a hundred miles from shore."

I knew the nor'easter was raging below us, the waves churning and choppy. They might not even be able to send out rescue. Survival would be very questionable.

"Anything, Neutrino," Toxicwasteman said in my ear. "I'll do anything."

I ignored him, trying to get my brain back on track, trying to tickle out that idea that was just below the surface.

"I'll turn myself in," he said, his words coming fast. "I've never lied to you, Neutrino, you know that. If you get this plane to land, I will turn myself in."

Time almost stopped. The yellow flames engulfing me no longer an annoyance. Neutrino shields and lasers. Fuel mixing with air and combusting. The fact that I hadn't melted the metal earbud Byte had given me. *Be the engine.*

"I have an idea," I shouted, "but I won't be able to talk anymore. Byte, I'm going to need you to slowly shuttle all the fuel over to this wing. Tom, get out here and now, I don't know if this will be enough."

"What are you going to do?" Tom asked, his voice sounding like a scared child's.

"I'm going to be the goddamn engine."

SUMMER 2025, NORTHERN ARIZONA

A RAVEN WAS CAWING IN THE DISTANCE AND PINE NEEDLES kept sticking into my feet as I stumbled around the forest feeling sorry for myself.

Don't get me wrong, I had plenty of reason to feel sorry for myself, but that still doesn't make it useful.

The slip-on slippers left enough of my feet exposed so that as I walked on the thick carpet of dried pine needles a sharp end would poke me every once in a while.

I had started down the rutted and rock-filled dirt road, but looking up at the clear blue sky, I worried about satellites and the powers that be looking at every image they could take of the area and noticing a bedraggled man with brown hair in a ratty blue robe and knowing it was me. So I wandered out among the pine trees not paying any attention to where I was going, plodding around downed trees, avoiding the occasional gambel oaks, getting my feet poked by pine needles.

The pine needles weren't the straw that broke the proverbial camel's back, but something like that.

I had no home. I had no life. My wife appeared to be furious with me. And our whisper of a plan was to do an interview with Diane Madison, the reporter that had caused me so many problems over the years.

It was ridiculous.

I was, it seemed, the most powerful man in the world and I had nothing, could do nothing, and was just hoping we weren't found before we left to, somehow, get to this interview.

A raven, high up in a dead pine tree that had shed its needles but was still standing, squawked at me, seeming to be insulted by my mere presence.

"Me too," I mumbled to him. I was insulted by my presence.

I think it's a trick of the human psyche, perhaps a flaw, that when we are up we think we will always be up, and when we are down we think we will always be down. Those extreme states feel like they will last forever, but they don't. They can't.

And I was down, thinking it could only get worse.

I sighed and sat on a boulder, light green moss clinging to one side, and raised my head to the sun. The life-giving sun. I took a deep breath and let out a long sigh. I didn't try to chase away the fears or the, let's face it, depression. I just breathed.

Above me I could hear squirrels scampering in a tree and that raven continued to squawk at me from the dead tree.

I narrowed my eyes and deepened my breath, slipping into that meditative state with much more ease than I had before. Maybe the old skills were coming back.

Images of Licia's balled fists and hard expression came to my mind and I let them, but I kept breathing. I saw Casita de Soledad with our adobe house and greenhouses nestled in the high desert. Images of the prison and Evan Saunders and the battle with the q-morph soldier flicked by. Gaia at the Hoover Dam. Toxicwasteman, Lightningirl, and I at Yellowstone flying above a buffalo stampede. Sarah the alien in her crashed alien craft, and more. Pictures of the war. Images of when Licia and I got married. My parents. Ashely

Long. Diane Madison. Chaosboy. Dr. Cheese. Quinn. On and on the images rattled through my brain and I breathed.

And then a new image came into my mind, of a future that I feared. Soldiers surrounding the old cabin armed with rifles and alien energy weapons. Knocking the door down. Killing Licia.

I kept breathing, but that image stuck, it wouldn't leave me. And it wasn't a ridiculous thought... well, the killing likely was. They would drag her off and throw her in the prison I was in so many years ago below Groom Lake at Area 51.

We shouldn't be apart right now, no matter how bruised we were from what happened yesterday. Licia and I, we are better together. That is the way it is for couples that work. For us, more so because of how our powers complement each other.

Without thinking about it, I got up, pine needles poking my feet, but I didn't care anymore. I walked back the way I came, except... I didn't know what way I had come.

The raven perched in the dead tree, squawking at me, seeming to tell me what a fool I was.

I was lost.

The thought of Licia's capture played in my head repeatedly like a skipping record. My heart pounding and my meditative deep breathing turning into desperate gasps as I started to sweat.

I couldn't think. I needed to get back to her. I thought of taking to the air, I could find the cabin easily that way, but that would risk exposing our position.

It seems silly in retrospect, but I was losing it. Nothing had happened, aside from getting lost, except in my mind. I was in a forest that was almost all pine trees, one portion of it looking very much like another. It was easy to lose your way if you didn't pay attention, and I most definitely had not.

19 / HERE IS WHERE IT GETS WEIRD

ME BECOMING NEUTRINOMAN, CHANGING ON A QUANTUM level from flesh and blood to a contained nuclear reaction, honestly, sounds like a bunch of mumbo-jumbo. I get that. I do. But you all have seen it. I can do it.

I can fly, shooting yellow jets out my feet and hands (a la Ironman in the comics) and out my butt (most definitely not Ironman). When I fly, I work in a similar way to a jet engine, I release pressurized gasses, the result of my internal nuclear reactions, in a controlled fashion (and I'm sure you see why the butt makes so much sense here). Those yellow jets are hot expanding gasses just like a rocket. Well... mostly. I mentioned when I first started writing about all of this that when I transform, I am governed more by quantum physics, than Newtonian physics, but you get the idea.

I can also go "elemental," losing my human form completely and exploding with nuclear force.

Until now, crammed in the engine of the 787, I hadn't found any states, besides flying and shields, between the human Neutrinoman and the elemental, exploding Neutrinoman.

And that is what came together in my mind. The neutrino shield meant I could create hard surfaces, which is why the earbud hadn't burned up, why my shoulder, pressed against that beam that joined the inner and outer portions of the jet engine hadn't melted. They hadn't because I hadn't wanted them to, and my form obeyed me. It created something akin to my shield so they could survive my touch.

Toxicwasteman was still talking in my ear, begging me to save his precious Gayle (aka Byte), promising to turn himself in if I did save her. No talk of aliens or how this world was his not theirs, just deep worry that he was about to lose something precious to him.

The flames from the leaking fuel combusting against my nuclear reaction were all around me, but I ignored them too. I focused on making my entire upper body firmer, less hot, covered in a "shield."

And it worked, the flames from the aerated fuel started occurring towards the back half of my body. That alien robot had disabled the jet engine's combustion chamber, where air and fuel mixed, burned, and released compressed gasses into the turbine which turned the front fan of the engine.

I had to become the combustion chamber. There was no turbine behind me, but if I could control the ignition of the fuel and the release of the gasses... well, that just might do it.

So I imagined myself as that combustion chamber. A shield all around my exterior, another shield, shaped like a funnel extending forth to capture the aerialized fuel and channel it deep into my body. There inside me, the fuel would combust and add to my nuclear reaction and expanding gases would pass out a small nozzle at the back of me.

I couldn't see myself as this transformation happened, and I am so glad. I think it would have so freaked me out and it wouldn't have worked. But I felt it. I felt myself filling up the space in a different way, getting larger, expanding. I saw a yellow, cone-shaped shield extending out in front of me. I felt the air enter and the fuel adding to my own internal reaction and then the gasses flying out behind me.

I had no legs, no hands, and even my sense of vision became vague, not that there was much to see in here.

I focused on taking in as much air as I could and releasing it out a narrow nozzle to produce as much thrust as possible.

"It's working," Byte's calm voice said in my ear. "Oh, my God, it's working. You're doing it."

Tom's voice was edged with manic relief. "I knew you could do it, Neutrino. I knew you could."

I couldn't talk, because I didn't have a mouth per se, but by some miracle of intention the earbud still worked, and I could hear them. And a thought burrowed into my head, a sick little worm of a thought. What if all of this, the robot, the disabled engine, the emergency, was arranged by Tom Tyree and Byte. What if Gayle wasn't her real name and this was just another one of the ways they were "training" me. Using Byte's simulations to plan this "attack" and manipulate me, to build me into what they wanted me to be.

"Wait. What happened?" Byte asked. "Our speed is going back down."

I felt the plane shudder as it hit some turbulence. I turned away from the thought. Now wasn't the time. And I focused on being the engine, combusting the fuel, keeping the plane in the air.

We were still a long way from land and I had no idea how long this would work.

20 / JUST A LITTLE FREAKOUT

My exhausted brain kept imagining more extreme scenarios as I ran through the forest in slippers and a robe trying to find the cabin, sweat trickling down my back, my breath coming fast.

As I imagined it, there would no longer be trained troops with alien weapons coming to capture us, but by the time I got back to the cabin it would be all ash, Licia having been obliterated by some missile.

The slip-on slippers were really slowing me down, so I took them off and subjected myself to constant pokes by pine needles, rocks, and sticks, but I could move faster.

It hurt, a lot. My recent transformation had been extreme, and I had come back with baby-soft feet, all my callouses gone, my body consuming any unneeded materials in the transformation, including those callouses.

It didn't matter. Licia was all that mattered. All that ever mattered. I ran, still not really thinking, hoping my feet would find their way back.

And then, in my mind, it wasn't even the military coming for her, it was one of the oblong, silver, alien spacecrafts, like Sarah had been flying when I met her. They had kidnapped Licia and were doing horrible experiments on her. A rogue alien leftover from the war exacting their revenge on me.

My exhausted brain kept spitting out scenarios as my feet got further banged up. I ran until... I was there at that dead pine tree again, the raven squawking at me.

I had run in a circle.

I sank to the ground. The truth was, I wasn't ready for this. While our exile had been difficult in many ways, it was also exactly what I needed. I had seen enough war and adventure, and while it was hard being so small after those crazy years, it was also safe.

It was a simple life building things and growing food, each day spent with the woman that makes this world make sense.

And I had ruined it.

I started gasping for breath. Even though I was sitting, my heart was racing. If I couldn't handle one simple thing, like being lost in the woods, how was I to handle getting Licia and I back to a life we could live? How was I to deal with the forces arrayed against us?

I had been fooling myself sitting in our adobe casita typing away about the past, feeling assured of our present, acting like I knew what the hell I was doing and what the hell had actually happened.

The raven continued to caw at me from its high-up perch on a dead limb as I struggled for air. I felt too hot in the old robe, but I had nothing else on so I kept it.

My sweat had soaked into that robe and the sweet smell of the forest, which I usually loved, seemed wrong.

This wasn't a prison, not like the one below Groom Lake, but I felt trapped. I couldn't escape.

The trees were closing in.

I couldn't breathe.

I had to get out of here.

I had to find Licia.

But in the state I was in, that was beyond me. I knew it. A dim part of me was still sane, aware that I was having a panic attack, that I needed to calm myself. That transforming into Neutrinoman and flying away would be foolish. That my paranoid imaginings of Licia's capture or murder were just that, imaginings. She was probably still pacing, stopping only long enough to take a sip of coffee.

I pulled a stick out from under my butt and crossed my legs. I closed my eyes most of the way and started observing my gasping breath. Not judging it, just observing it. The raven kept cawing, which I tried not to fight. I let my breaths slip into the same rhythm as the caws. Still too fast, but slower.

I breathed, not trying to chase my demons away, but not playing with them anymore either.

I breathed. It was the only thing I could do.

INTERLUDE 2

I'm having trouble here. Yes, I'm lost in the forest, desperate to find Licia, worried that I've made another colossal blunder. But that's not what I'm talking about. I'm having trouble writing about this.

I do worry about what people will think of me. Neutrinoman lost in the forest, depressed, in an old bathrobe and slippers about to lose his mind. But that's not it either.

(Well, I could be fooling myself about this, but I don't *think* that's it. I can't really tell this story without looking fairly silly at times.)

What I really worry about is that I'm now boring you. That you don't want to hear about the personal struggles. You want to hear about superpowers and daring do and alien threats and maybe even a few grand romantic gestures to sweep my beautiful superpowered wife off of her feet.

You might have noticed, but I usually write these "interludes" as a conversation between Licia and I. Because these usually are conversations and this one, in fact, was a conversation we had. But I'm not going to write it like that.

For one, I can't tell you where we are. Our future is still uncertain, and it would be foolish to even hint at our location and I don't want to fake it like I did for the last interlude.

Also, Licia is not in the mood. She's still reading these chapters as I write them and it's clear now that it's not going to work if another one of them feels like when we were safe, if not content, at Casita de Soledad. Now is not that time for an adorable interaction between us—the loss of our home is too fresh.

But I digress. And perhaps the digression was boring too but hear me out. Please.

I'm writing about these small, human moments because they happened... Well, not *just* because they happened, but because they are important. My struggles with PTSD probably aren't what you are after here, but it's real. I won't detail every last piece of it, every time I struggle with shame and guilt, but my humanity, as demonstrated by my simple freak out in the forest, is very important to me.

Just because I can rocket into orbit at will doesn't mean I don't have the most down-to-earth problems.

And here I am breaking all the storytelling rules. "Show don't tell" they say. Okay, then, I'll get back to showing, but bear with me a while I'm just so very human.

I WASN'T ME ANYMORE, THE FUEL AND AIR MIXTURE funneling into me through my "head" combusting inside of my "body" and hot gasses spewing forth out a narrow nozzle at my back end. I had no head. No legs. No arms.

I had a vague sense of sight and I could hear just fine, Byte giving me updates on our progress, but my mind wasn't the same.

When I transform into Neutrinoman, I am "me." I mean, except for the flying and neutrino bolts and stuff, I still feel like me. I can't smell, and my sense of touch is numb and imprecise, but I have my memories and my thoughts. I feel like me.

When I go elemental and explode, I am most definitely gone. The elemental me guided by whatever intent I had before, but I am most definitely not conscious. My mind, which is present in my normal Neutrinoman q-morph form is absent as an elemental.

There, crammed into the 787's jet engine, I wasn't me, but I wasn't gone either. I was something more primal, hungry, fierce, single-minded.

I was the fire, seeking fuel, reveling in the flames. Eating. I felt strong and powerful. I felt indestructible. I felt so very sure of myself.

That last part... I have to tell you, it felt so good. After my time in the q-morph prison and being so clingy with Licia, feeling like I was alone when she wasn't with me, this was something I really needed.

I've never been the kind of person that felt sure of themselves. Ever. I doubt myself. All the time. Quite the opposite of Tom Tyree, who never has any doubt. But then again, he's a sociopath and I am not, so there is that.

"You're doing great, Nik," Byte's computerized voice said in my ear. I was back to thinking of her as Byte. Part of it was the primal state I was in, the other part was my doubt that Gayle with a "y" was her real name, that this whole thing wasn't some crazy Tom Tyree training program.

"I think I've got the rate down," she continued. "I'm moving fuel over from the starboard fuel tank. We're hitting a lot of turbulence and still losing altitude, but at this rate, we'll make it back to JFK."

It was the nor'easter that was the cause of the turbulence, but I was the engine, I was fire, I cared not for such things. I couldn't answer, and it was fairly miraculous that I could still hear her, that I had preserved my sense of hearing in this transformation and kept the earbud in place.

She was going to continue to supply me with fuel and that made me happy. As much as fire can be happy.

"I should get there a few minutes before you get back over land," Toxicwasteman said in my ear. The manic relief from earlier was gone from his voice. But I didn't like him. His voice, although it was real and not synthesized like Byte's, grated on me. I didn't trust it. I didn't need his help. I was the fire. I was the engine. I could do this.

"Wait," Byte said. "Oh hell. There's another one of those robots. It just activated. Nik, can you do something? It is crawling out the hole you made in the fuselage and is heading towards the port wing."

They didn't understand. I wasn't Nik. I was the fire. I was the engine. If I stopped being the fire the plane would fall—I had a strong sense of purpose. And, if I stopped being the fire, I would lose my sense of purpose and confidence—I knew that feeling was special and worth keeping.

But there was enough of my mind left to know that the alien robot was on my wing and could interfere with my purpose.

I let go of being the engine, so I could do battle with this foul robot, but I wasn't quite back to being myself.

THE RAVEN WAS THE KEY. ONCE I CALMED DOWN, SITTING ON the pine needles, feeling the panic and trying not to judge it, focusing on my breath, the regular caw-caw of the raven slowly becoming reassuring.

I heard a bird in a tree in the middle of a forest on a beautiful summer's day, me sitting and breathing, letting my imagination run wild, but not focusing on it. Just the breath. Just the in and out, feeling the air pass through my nostrils.

And then I remembered. I heard that same raven cawing when I left the cabin. It was distant and to the left of the road. I slowly rose, keeping my breath steady, my eyes not quite open all the way, and walked back, keeping that sound of the raven to my right and behind me.

It didn't take long, not in that state, time didn't really matter. Soon I was back to the cabin, the sun shining, the gentle breeze bringing the vanilla scent of the pines to me. The cabin was intact, there were no soldiers, no alien spaceships, no obvious threats.

But then I blinked open my eyes all the way, my heart starting to thump again. Licia was there. She was furious. We were still in this untenable position.

I took a deep breath and shook it off. If Licia was all that really mattered, then I best act like it.

I walked in and found Licia slumped in the rocking chair rubbing at the tears on her cheeks and sniffing. My wife is strong, so strong, that it's hard for me to see her like this. Not that she doesn't get to feel her feelings, not at all, it just scares me when the strongest person I know doesn't appear to be strong.

My stomach fell, and I felt like I was standing on the edge of a cliff looking over. I swayed as if I were really on that cliff, feeling dizzy and realizing that I was starving, my blood sugar well on the way to an epic crash.

But I didn't move. I stared, her brown eyes not meeting mine.

"I'm sorry," I whispered. And I was, but the words felt hollow and wholly inadequate.

"I'm angry," she said, her tone quiet but fierce.

I nodded. I wanted to go to her, to touch her, to hold her, to beg her for her forgiveness. But I didn't. I knew that wasn't the best thing right now. If I did that it would be about me and not about her.

"I'm sorry," I repeated. It felt even more hollow this time.

She rose, biting her lip, her arms hugging her chest, her eyes finally meeting mine. "I am so angry, Nik, I want to burn this forest down. I want to break everything I can find. I want to lay waste to the world. I want to..."

Her voice faltered, and she took a deep breath and sighed.

I looked down. I could not meet the fierceness in her eyes. I had only shame, and shame is no defense against anger.

"But I'm not mad at *you*, Nik." She was suddenly next to me, less than an arm's length away, but she didn't reach out.

"What?" I looked up, and even though she wasn't Lightningirl, I saw the eyes of a goddess. The fire, the fierceness was there, but so was compassion. Tears were slowly rolling down her cheeks.

"After the war was over," she began, quietly, but her words gaining strength, "they trapped us in their legal net, they coerced us into signing the Accords, and then they forced us into our desert exile, but first they planted a bomb underneath us and then they watched our every move, listened to our every word.

"I'm angry, Nik. I'm furious... but not at you." She paused, looking down, and then took my hand and squeezed it. "I grieve our loss, our beautiful home, our simple life, but I'm grateful the charade is over. I'm not going down without a fight. *We're* not going down quietly. We obeyed the rules, they did not."

I nodded, feeling her anger sparking my own, starting to wear away at my shame.

She shook her head, her long hair waving behind her. "I don't know if we'll survive, I don't know how we find a life after this, but..." And then she was in my arms and I held her tight.

"But we will do this together," I said, finishing her sentence.

I felt her nod and held her tight, hoping we would be enough for this challenge, hoping we would find a way.

23 / BEAST MODE

BEAST MODE. THAT'S WHAT I'VE COME TO THINK OF THE STATE I was in after I stopped being the engine and flew to meet the robot threat.

Beast mode. I was more myself than when I was sucking on fuel and taking the place of the airplane's engine, but I wasn't my normal self yet. I was bigger, eight feet tall, with a flatter face and huge hands. My mind was in a state to match my body, just like when Quinn turned into the Hammer and attacked Gaia at the Hoover Dam. I was aggressive and angry. This was my plane, and the silver alien robot was clinging to it, attacking it. I didn't want to be here, I wanted the simple life of being the engine, and I was angry about it.

I spotted the foot-long robot scuttling on the port wing as I flew. The clouds were thick and grey, laced with flashes of lightning, the wind blowing hard against me, but I didn't care. I had an enemy and a mission. A simple one. Preserve the plane and destroy the robot.

There was some benefit to thinking less, or rather, not over-thinking like I often do. My neutrino form changed quickly, did what I needed it to do without any fuss. No deep breaths, no concentration. I was elemental enough that I didn't need to "think" about controlling myself.

Look at it this way. When you learn to ride a bike, you have to really think about it. It's awkward and difficult and you fall a lot. After you learn, when you really are riding a bike, you aren't thinking about it, you are just doing it.

In beast mode I was just being Neutrinoman, not thinking about it.

In my ear, I could hear Byte's computerized voice, but I wasn't listening. She was saying something about the loss of speed, the time until the plane crashed into the ocean, things like that. My brain, such as it was, took it in, but it really just added to the urgency I was already feeling.

The robot had placed itself on the middle of the wing about sixteen feet from the fuselage and sprouted some kind of proboscis and poked it through the wing, its head starting a rapid sawing motion.

I wrapped my form in a protective shield, except for the jets coming out of my legs and hands. I did not want to harm the plane, *my* plane. I flew fast directly towards the robot.

As I got closer, I saw that the proboscis was serrated, it literally was a saw and as I approached, it reached its target and fuel started flying up from the wing, that fuel hitting me, rolling off the shielded parts of me and igniting at my hands and feet, a long tail of flame trailing behind me.

If the beast-me was mad before, now it was furious. The robot had damaged *my* plane. I flew up out of the way of the fuel and zoomed in front of the wing, timing my approach carefully, which was not easy. The plane was slowing, but it was still going several hundred miles per hour. It's not like I could just land on the wing (neutrino jets, you know). So, I zoomed just ahead of the wing, cut all jets, tightened my shields, twisted around, and landed on the wing and slid right towards the robot.

This is the kind of "just riding the bike" maneuver I couldn't have made if I had been thinking about it. It was instinct.

But the robot wasn't there when I slid to the mid wing, it had danced aside, its wide silver feet somehow sticking to the metal skin of the wing and I slid past and off the wing, the robot resuming its position and its sawing.

I tried again, flying ahead, cutting the jets, tightening my shield and landing on the wing, but the little guy was too fast. It just moved out of the way.

My anger mounted and my form grew bigger as I became more of a beast.

You must have seen the videos some of the passengers shot as I got bigger, more primal and more elemental. The yellow neutrino swirls are there, but blurred by the translucent shield that covered my body. Normally, looking at me as Neutrinoman, you wouldn't call me muscular. If you were being kind, you'd say I have well-defined muscles. The same is not true for beast mode. My form ripples with muscles, even though that doesn't make a lot of sense. I am a controlled nuclear reaction, I don't literally have muscles, but my form follows my mind and my mind was a lot less Nik Nichols and a lot more the Incredible Hulk.

I roared in rage as I slid off the wing. This wasn't working. I had to think, apply logic, be rational, but... beast mode, you know.

A third time I flew ahead, dropped onto the wing and slid down to where the robot had just been, but this time I lunged out with my arm and clipped the sucker as my fist tried to close on it. I tore off two arms and slid off the wing.

I glanced at the robot's arms as I briefly fell. They appeared to be metal, shiny silver, but as I watched them, they changed, they melted, turning into this dark purple liquid that began sizzling against my shield, like acid eating through metal.

The first robot I had encountered had taken samples of me.

Even with my blunted intellect, I saw this as related. The purple liquid metal, or whatever it was, was designed to hurt me.

And it was painful, a fierce burning sensation even when I had little sense of touch as Neutrinoman.

As I fell, I yelled at the purple stain and my hands they... Well, my hands exploded. Just a little bit, just in the area of the liquid. The shield I had been producing absorbed back into my neutrino form and then the pain got bad. But it was only a moment and the yellow of my palms got blindingly bright—although I didn't have physical eyes, so it didn't blind me—and small explosions erupted expelling the foreign substance.

Another new ability courtesy of beast mode and not over-thinking everything. This didn't take long, only a few seconds, and I flew back to the plane, my anger even greater. When I got to the plane, the damn robot had grown its arms back and was sawing again, the amount of fuel leaking out becoming substantial.

I had to try something else. I had to think. My plane was going to fall into the ocean and that was not acceptable. Not at all.

I flew forward in front of the wing, but this time I twisted my neck and watched the robot. As I cut my jets, I noticed it pulling its saw out of the plane and moving to scuttle farther out on the wing. As I fell, I used my right hand to change my trajectory, keeping the neutrino jet small and pointed away from the wing.

This time I ran right into the robot and knocked it off the plane.

I smiled as I watched it disappear into the grey of the clouds, just a brief moment of victory, and then I was flying behind my plane seeing the huge fuel leak and finally having enough of a mind to hear Byte's words.

"...got to stop the leak now or we're going to crash. Nik, we don't have much time, can you hear me?"

The clouds below us thinned and then were gone and I could see the roiling Atlantic Ocean below. Byte was right, we didn't have much time. I had to find a way to stop the leak and be the engine at the same time.

SUMMER 2025, NORTHERN ARIZONA

I VIVIDLY REMEMBER *THE INCREDIBLE HULK* TV SHOW starring Bill Bixby. That sad and plaintive piano playing at the end, time after time seeing Bruce Banner with an old coat and a backpack along some lonely road with his thumb out, trying to get a ride to the next place, the next chapter, the next chance at redemption.

I was born in 1974, so I was seven and eight watching the show towards the end of its run with my father. It wasn't my mother's kind of thing, so the two of us would watch it together on the old brown couch while he drank a beer and I sipped on a root beer. Every week as I watched, I was a little bit conflicted. I was, of course, hoping that Bruce could find the peace that he craved, but I was dubious that he would like his life without the Hulk being a part of him. He did good with the monster within, he had power with the monster within, he would have been dead so many times over without that monster transforming him at the most dire of times.

My mind was thinking of Bruce Banner as I stuck my thumb

out on a twisting section of blacktop that ran through the pine tree forest of the Kaibab Plateau north of the Grand Canyon. Licia was next to me, her brown eyes staring up at the blue sky, lost in thought.

We had left that day I had gotten lost. After breakfast we put on backpacks and started walking north through the forest. The cabin was remote, but it being summer there was plenty going on in the forest. ATVs ripping along the dirt roads, campers set up here and there. But we avoided everyone and had camped under the stars the previous night, eating cold beans and getting up in the morning and making it here to 89A.

Licia had a wig on now, short blond hair, and I had on sunglasses and an old cowboy hat we had found in the cabin. We looked dirty and bedraggled, which we let be so it could add to the disguise.

We had a plan... well, something of a plan. The interview with Diane Madison was thirteen days off. Our plan was to lie low, get out of the area, keep moving, and show up to the interview and tell the world what was going on. We needed to get a burner cell phone so we could have Byte arrange a few things for us. It wasn't much, but it was a plan.

As I stood there, my thumb out, the cooling breeze welcome, my nose full of the sweet scent of the pine trees, I thought about Bruce Banner and his quest to rid himself of the Hulk. Would I be better without Neutrinoman, living a simple life during these difficult times? If this was a TV show about our story, would the music playing be lonely and plaintive? Would the camera zoom out showing the remoteness of our location making the task in front of us seem that much larger? Illustrate how far we have fallen.

I smiled as the thoughts bounced around my head, because the answer was easy. No, the music wouldn't be lonely because while there was a huge challenge in front of us, there was an "us." Licia was here. She's not going anywhere. I have a partner, someone that makes me better and stronger.

And then the smile faded. I'm not alone, but I couldn't see a way out of this, a way for us to have a life, be in this world, be happy. I just couldn't.

So maybe sad music, maybe plaintive, but not lonely.

FALL 2006, OVER THE ATLANTIC OCEAN

The waves were dark, tipped with white foam, the winds of the nor'easter churning them into a froth. The plane bucked in the winds as I flew towards the port wing with its gushing fuel leak, Byte chattering in my ear.

"Tom is still a ways off," her calm, computerized voice said. "You've got to stop the leak. You've got to get our speed back up. There will be no rescue in these conditions."

Byte's voice was calm and computerized because she was not actually speaking but sending her synthesized voice to my earbud with her mind. But her sentences had gotten short and to the point. Even in beast mode, I could feel her anxiety and didn't need her encouragement. This was my plane, my fuel that was leaking. I wanted nothing more than to be the simple purposeful engine again.

And it was the engine that I summoned... no, that's not the right word. I didn't summon the more elemental me, it was still there, right below the surface, eager to return.

I can't watch the videos of this. It makes me profoundly uncomfortable to think of what I became. But I will do my best to describe it.

The leak was a third of the way out the port wing. As the huge beast-mode Neutrinoman flew closer, his head became large, his body swelling behind him, his mouth opening and extending like a toothless crocodile.

Okay... okay... I am describing myself in the third person. I did say "profoundly uncomfortable" up above, didn't I? Okay, let me try again.

My mouth extended and elongated as I approached the wing, my body fully shielded except for my hands and feet where the fuel ignited and a long flame blasted out into the wind.

It didn't last long. My now huge mouth clamped down on the wing and contained the leak, the fuel pooling inside my form. My legs had fused together, and I was a yellow tube with a tapering back end. The top of my "head" grew, like some sort of weird tumor and then it opened up so it looked something like an air intake on a muscle car. And that's what it was. Flames started shooting out my back end, as I combined the fuel with air and combusted it inside of me.

The flames were yellow and long, but as I got the mixture right, the flames virtually disappeared in the air behind me shimmered with heat.

I was a yellow cylinder clamped onto the wing. There was nothing recognizably human about me. If you saw a picture of it without knowing the story, the yellow motes and swirls beneath the translucent shield would remind you of me, but you wouldn't say, "Hey, is that Neutrinoman?" There was no "man" involved anymore.

But I was happy. No, that's not the right word. I wasn't really capable of happiness, but I was whole and complete with a purpose I knew I was fulfilling. I was the engine. I was the fire. I could feel the plane speed up as it continued to buck against the wind. There was hope.

I had a sense of sight, but I could see all around me. Below the plane to the churning ocean, above the plane to the dark clouds, and I could see the passengers staring out the window at me. At first, as I transformed, their looks were looks of horror and fright. When they saw it was working, those faces changed to hope. And this pleased me deeply.

"...we've lost a lot of fuel," Byte was saying. By some instinct I was still preserving that earbud, still hearing her, even though I didn't have a head much less an ear. The metal earbud was still embedded in the front portion of my engine form, still working. "But we don't have enough fuel now. I hope you can hear me. I hope you can find a way."

IT TOOK HOURS FOR SOMEONE TO STOP FOR US. 89A HERE RUNS from Jacob Lake to Fredonia, not exactly a major thoroughfare. It was a lovely summer day with the temperatures among the pines up in the seventies, the sky filled with high, thin clouds blunting that startling blue color you often get at eight thousand feet in elevation.

Licia and I talked, but not about much of anything. We remembered some trips together to this area in happier times, but we didn't go too far with that. These were not happy times and we were still processing what had happened.

Or, at least, I was. I could still hear the piano playing the theme from *The Incredible Hulk* as I stuck my thumb out for the intermittent vehicles roaring by. Since Licia and I couldn't get lost in conversation or nostalgia, it was my way of band-aiding the psychological wound until it could be attended to... whatever the hell that means. As I write this, I have more distance on what happened, a lot more perspective, but it's still a difficult thing to bear.

So my mind is occupied with Bruce Banner on his lonely quest to free himself from the inner monster, instead of Nik Nichols who just got his home vaporized and has no idea how he and his wife will ever find peace.

The couple that stopped for us looked to be in their seventies, with snow-white hair, wrinkled faces, and a fair amount of extra weight. They were driving an old RV, the kind built on a van frame, not one of those huge behemoths.

"Where y'all headed?" the man asked from the rolled down driver's side window as we walked up.

"West," I said, because I had to say something, and it was the way the road was headed.

"Just to Fredonia," Licia added. When the man's wrinkled forehead furrowed further, she added, "It's only thirty miles down the road."

"Well hop on in then," he said with a smile, his head nodding towards the other side of the RV.

"Fredonia?" I whispered to Licia as we walked around the back.

She nodded. "We have to pick up something there."

I wanted to ask her what she's talking about but there wasn't any time. And then I was worried. We spent all this time hiking and standing by the side of the road and we didn't talk about the next step except me asking Licia which way we should go and her telling me west. She had a plan after what happened at Casita de Soledad, she still had a plan now, and I still had no idea what it was.

We were both still in shock by what had happened, but I needed to do better. We needed to start acting like a team again.

"Welcome aboard the Polar Express," the white-haired woman said from the passenger's seat. She had bright blue eyes and a nice smile. "I'm Jean, this my partner in crime, Alan." She extended her hand which was soft and warm. I shook hands with Alan, but didn't say anything, my mind slipping.

I needed to introduce myself, but I couldn't use my name. We should have talked about this too.

"Thank you for stopping," Licia said, a big smile on her face. She still had on her sunglasses and her shoulder-length blond wig. "You are so kind. My name is Lee, this is Neil."

"What are you two doing out on this lonely stretch of road?" Alan asked.

Licia laughed, it was quiet and shy. "Well, Neil here bet me that we couldn't make it from our home in Yuma all the way to my uncle's house in Fredonia just by hitchhiking."

I nodded, warming to the charade. I didn't want to be myself right now, so why not be this "Neil"? "Yes, sir," I said. "I was convinced that we wouldn't find enough kind people like yourselves after... well, you know." I ended in a shrug.

Jean nodded her head and sighed. "That alien war was an awful thing and all that terrible finger pointing afterward. It didn't always bring out the best in us."

"And I was sure we would," Licia said, her smile bright, but I knew she was faking it. "And I'm about to win that bet." She turned and punched me in the shoulder. It looked playful, but it hurt.

"Well, buckle up, you two," Alan said, starting the van up. "We've got to win Lee a bet. The Polar Express will get you there!"

Jean smiled. "We call it that because... well, we're headed towards Alaska and we're not very creative... or geographically accurate."

Licia laughed and this time it hurt in my gut. It wasn't a real laugh, she was playing a part. What did we have to laugh about?

FALL 2006, OVER THE ATLANTIC OCEAN

TIME SLIPPED PAST IN THE ODDEST WAY AS I SUCKED THE FUEL out of the wing, mixed it with air, ignited it in my body, and spewed the hot gasses forth keeping the damaged 787 aloft.

I was aware of the passage of time, the chop of the sea below, the spasms of turbulence that shook my plane, the looks of the passengers as they would stare out the window, the worry written clearly on their faces. But I wasn't aware of how much time had passed, if that makes any sense. I was not concerned with the future or the past. Just the now. The mixing of fuel and air, the ignition, the flames, the thrust.

Byte would talk in my "ear" from time to time, encouraging me. Toxicwasteman chimed in a couple of times reiterating his promise to turn himself in if I got the plane back to land. Their words, their pleas, felt familiar, felt like they should mean something, but I didn't care. I couldn't reply and continued executing my purpose.

Until...

The fuel ran out.

And my purpose was no longer achievable.

And land was not yet in sight.

And the plane started to head towards those stormy seas.

That's the thing about being the engine. What are you if you can't do your job? Just an empty container longing for fuel and air. Just a lifeless cylinder that has no purpose.

I wasn't fully elemental—thankfully—but I was far enough on that side of the spectrum that at first the lack of fuel was puzzling and then it was infuriating, but I was stuck. I had been the engine for so long, loved the single-minded focus and purpose, that I was lost. I didn't know how to change back into Neutrinoman, much less Nik Nichols.

"Nik, please hear me," the ever-calm voice of Byte said in my ear. "Come back to us. Please. Can you hear me, Nik?"

She didn't call me Neutrinoman or even Neutrino like Toxi-cwasteman would have. She called me by my real name. My human name. My mundane earthling name.

"Tom is still ten minutes out," she continued, the plane bucking violently against the force of the storm. "The airports are closed. The coast guard is at dock. We need to get this airplane to land. Nik? Can you hear me, Nik?"

The dark, churning ocean was coming near. My plane was falling, it would die. And that is the word that I felt, "die." My plane. My failure. My death.

But I was just an engine without fuel, what could I do?

"Honey, it's me." It was Licia's voice in my ear now. "I'm sorry I left. I should have been there with you." Unlike Byte, her voice was normal, filled with an emotion I couldn't quite identify in my current state. "Can you hear me, Nik? Byte has told me what you've done, what an incredible thing you managed to do getting everyone this far. But you are so close. I know you, Nik. I know you can do this."

Her voice was smooth, too smooth, something she would do when she was trying to hide her worry. But that voice was so familiar that with each time she said my name, I felt myself return a little bit more. A little less engine, a bit more Nik.

"I love you, Nik, you know that, right?" Licia asked, her voice getting thick. She was worried, but why? I couldn't understand that, but I wanted to. "We've been so busy lately, maybe I haven't said it enough. No matter what happens here, I love you. Do you hear me, Nik? Nik!" Her voice was edging higher. Was she worried that I would never recover, that in being the engine I would go down with the plane. That I would die, too.

Those were barely thoughts in my state, but it was what she was worried about. I was doing things the military had never conceived of. Byte didn't have enough data to run an accurate simulation, but the ones she had run had worried her enough to contact Licia.

"Remember the first time we kissed," Licia said with a sniff. "At the winery with Oak Creek below us, the grape vines planted on the hill above us. Do you remember, Nik? Can we take a break from all this recruiting and go back there? There's a place near there that has cabins. We could go incognito and just forget the world for a few days. Just you and me. Just us."

Licia was waxing romantic and the waves were getting close, too close. Licia wasn't the romantic and planes fly in the air, they don't go into the ocean. My plane... no, "the" plane was going to go down. I had to do something.

"Nik?" Licia said, and I could hear the tears in her voice. "Come on, Nik? Say something. Please."

I can't tell you how I did it. How I stopped being the engine and started being Neutrinoman again. How I left that simplicity of a single-minded purpose and returned to my decidedly difficult and chaotic life. It was Licia, for sure, giving me something I wanted more than being the engine, but I can't tell you "how." When I go from flesh and blood to my q-morph form it is like a switch, an act of will. Here, one moment I was the engine and the next I was

Neutrinoman falling towards the ocean feeling weak and disoriented.

"Lower the landing gear," I said as I flew back towards the plane. There was shouting in my ear, both Byte and Licia speaking their relief, but I didn't have time to listen. The plane was only hundreds of feet above the churning water and land was nowhere in sight.

I WAS DOING MY BEST ATLAS IMPRESSION, NOT HOLDING UP the entire earth, just the plane, my shielded shoulders crammed against the axel between the front two tires of the port landing gear while I thrusted with my hands, my feet, my butt... with everything I had.

I wasn't trying to be the engine, I was just trying to slow the fall, make the plane lighter, hoping Byte and the pilot could use that to get us farther.

I wasn't in beast mode but back to regular old Neutrinoman and I was running out of power. I had been transformed for ninety minutes or so, expending energy the whole time, I could feel my nuclear reaction waning.

And still the dark oceans churned, slowly getting closer, the wind blew and the plane bucked and I thrusted.

"Will you come work for me?" I asked Byte. Licia wasn't on the line anymore, she was back to helping out at the power plant having gotten me back to myself. She was physically taking the place of some burned out transformers, powering hundreds of thousands of homes to keep them warm during a blizzard in the Pacific Northwest. She had more important things to do than to talk to me.

"What?" Byte asked. I was so sick of her calm, computerized voice.

"Surely you knew," I said.

"I don't know that I do now."

"That's why I wanted to meet you. To ask you to come work for me at Heroes Incorporated."

And I guess this might seem strange. I'm in the middle of a crisis and I'm trying to recruit a q-morph onto the team. And it was strange. But I hadn't asked her when we had been on board, having the big fat panic attack I was having, and right then I really needed a distraction. I didn't want to think about how hard this was, or how I was probably going to fail, or about how Licia had to stop helping so many to help me.

"That is interesting," she said.

"I would be hiring Gayle—sorry, I don't know your last name—not Byte. Your identity would remain secret. You would head up the IT department, ensure that the military is keeping their end of the bargain, get us some simulations up and running to help guide our decision making."

There was silence and, frankly, that wasn't good for me. "You could help liaison with strategic partners," I added. I didn't come out and say it, that I wanted her to coordinate with Toxicwasteman and his gang at LoVE. For a few reasons. I had been through enough to worry that we might be overheard, even though this was Byte I was communicating with. But mostly because I didn't want to say it out loud.

I mean, I believed that we would need everyone to defeat the aliens if they came back. What I didn't want to admit out loud is how deeply Tom Tyree had influenced me.

"You can't have her!" Toxicwasteman said in my ear, his voice no longer calm, no longer pleading, but full of energy and anger.

So that was the delay—she was talking to him.

"I'm not asking you," I shot back, a groan in my voice as the weight of what I was doing became difficult to bear. Planes are heavy, you know. "Let the lady speak for herself."

"Forget it, Neutrino, it's not going to happen." There was an implied "she's mine" in what he said in the way he said it, and that made me angry.

I wanted to shout back, tell him how Byte was not his property, how she was a powerful woman and could make up her own mind, that he should butt out and let me assemble my team, this whole Heroes Incorporated being something he catalyzed.

But I didn't. I heard how that would play out in my head, two men talking about a woman and what they thought was best for her. If I was ever in such a conversation and Licia ever found out... well, let's just say that it wouldn't go well for me. But that wasn't the reason I held my tongue. My mother is the reason. While she was often the definition of a helicopter mom, had a way too intense love of tchotchkes, and changed her hair color way too often, she was a strong woman. She ran my father's accounting business, doing everything but the accounting. She helped my grandparents, in their eighties then, remain in their home by doing everything they couldn't do anymore. She volunteered at the soup kitchen and had helped my uncle—my father's brother who she didn't like at all —through his cancer treatments. She didn't go to college. She didn't have any flashy skills or talents, and yet she, single-handedly, held the family together and made it work.

As the silence went on, and these thoughts flitted through my head, I really missed my mom and would like nothing better than to have her doing or saying something that, like mothers were so good at doing, deeply embarrassed me. Since my time in prison, since we started Heroes Incorporated, I had been staying away. I didn't want to see the worried look on her face as she asked me how I was doing, insisted I wasn't eating enough, told me that I should slow down some.

And I should slow down. Get away with Licia, go spend some time with my mom, help my dad tinker with his Charger.

But the potential alien attack, the needs of forming a team to meet them, it seemed like I was always carrying this huge weight, and right then, I literally was carrying a huge weight, a 787 airplane.

"Gayle," I said quietly, hearing the emotion of all that had just run through my head clearly in my voice. "I need you."

That was it. Three words. Just the truth.

I AM A ROMANTIC, THAT IS CERTAINLY CLEAR BY NOW, BUT I also live in the real world.

My world was walking behind my wife as she marched east down Pratt Street in Fredonia, Arizona. Her steps metronomically steady, her head straight ahead, her voice silent. The backpack made it hard to tell, but I'm pretty sure her back was straight and I could see that her fists were balled up.

Gone was the pleasant chitchat with Jean and Alan who had let us off in front of the Grand Canyon Hotel, the faded red fifties-style sign out front topped awkwardly with a wagon wheel.

I'm romantic enough to believe with all my heart that I am a better person with Licia, that she makes my life worth living, that I would literally be dead a dozen times over without her. But—and here's the "real world" part—I didn't feel that connection then. Not since Project Vulcan vaporized our home. We were not on the same wavelength, or however you'd like to put it. We were a couple, we were together, but we were not one.

And when you're used to feeling that togetherness, it's very disorienting when you no longer feel it.

What I wanted to do was pepper her with questions, find out exactly how much escape planning she did without breathing a word to me.

Don't get me wrong, I'm glad she did it. But it's hard to feel your partner is your partner when this level of deception comes to light. Maybe deception is the wrong word. She didn't actively deceive me—I don't think—but she sure did hide a lot from me.

After ten minutes, the small, scattered houses fell away and the road continued through flat desert, short weeds trying to survive in the reddish, sandy soil.

Another minute or two and we were standing in front of the Fredonia Cemetery, a generous plot of land out here separated from the rest of Fredonia, as if the growth of the town was stunted and it never grew out this far like in most towns.

The cemetery had a low chain-link fence that met a short flagstone wall on either side of the entrance. A wrought-iron gateway framed the entrance with the letters spelling "FREDONIA CEMETERY" backdropped by the darkening sky as the sun headed towards the horizon behind us. Below the entryway was, and I'm not kidding here, a cattle guard. Most of the plot was empty with several rows on the far side green-brown with struggling grass and some granite and flowers sticking up. Nice of them to protect the grass and the flowers from cows, but I guess it says something about Fredonia that they needed to.

We were not there long. I helped Licia pull a large limestone rock up, just on the other side of the wall. She dug, pulled out a small metal box, and stowed it in her pack. We put the rock back and soon we were marching back west on Pratt Street.

"I appreciate you not asking all the questions I know are driving you mad right now," she said from in front of me.

I smiled. There was distance between us and that feels profoundly uncomfortable, but my wife still knew me and I knew her. "No problem," I said, although it was anything but. "I do hope there is room for food in our itinerary soon, though."

She chuckled and shook her head, her metronomic pace not wavering one little bit.

It wasn't much, just a second of almost laughter, but on a day like today it was a lot.

FALL 2006, OVER THE ATLANTIC OCEAN

TOXICWASTEMAN CAME ROARING IN, A SICKLY GREEN STREAK with a trail of coal-black smoke behind him.

He was mad.

He was just in time.

The churning ocean was a hundred feet below us and my Atlas impression was just about to end. It had been radio silent since I had tried to recruit Byte, told her that I needed her. I was pretty sure they were having their own discussion and I doubted that Toxicwasteman was using his inside voice.

His swirling green face was hard as he took position on the starboard landing gear between the two inner wheels just like me and started doing his own Atlas impression. As he flew in to take his position, I did notice that his upper body, where it pressed against the axle of the landing gear, had a translucent green layer. His version of a shield. He was a contained chemical reaction while I was a contained nuclear reaction... we were more alike than I liked to admit.

. . .

"Don't talk," Byte's English-accented, computerized voice said in my ear. "Just listen, please. He's mad, but he'll get over it. Thank you for your kind offer, but I must politely decline."

"No," I said it quietly and then I turned and shouted it at Toxicwasteman. "No!"

He turned, the strain on his face obvious, from our effort to keep this 787 aloft, yes, but maybe from what I was asking. His pleas earlier made it clear that he needed her. The psychopathic villain needed someone and at first that had heartened me. But now, it seemed that he needed her to be exclusively his. Byte's assertion that "he's not the jealous type" in the LoVE base near the Grand Canyon had either not been correct or something had changed.

"Care to elaborate, Neutrino?" His eyes were hooded and his trademark wolfish grin was not decorating his lean face.

I hesitated. I didn't want to have a fight about Byte with her listening, with two men talking about her like she wasn't present. But what could I do?

"No," I repeated. "You don't get to decide for another human. No."

"I didn't decide, she did." His upper lip curled back as he groaned from the effort, green flames and black smoke pouring out his hands, his feet, and yes, his butt.

"I don't believe you."

"Please let it go," Byte said in my ear.

"No!" I shouted.

When I had met Byte in the LoVE base, when they were trying to recruit me, when she tried to seduce me, she had told me how she had gone mad after her transformation, how she got locked up and Tom Tyree had found her and helped her. I remember the look she had given Tom had been one of love and admiration. But what I was seeing now disturbed me.

"All this time. All this effort," I shouted at Toxicwasteman.

"You've been trying to mold me into a weapon that can defeat the aliens. I'm sure Byte's simulations are nearly certain they're coming back, it's not like the human race is going to suddenly get its act together. And yet here I am trying to form my team, trying to get *your* Heroes Incorporated off the ground, and you're blocking me. Why?"

He looked at me, his eyes wider, his face slack, almost innocent, and then he looked away.

"Why?" I shouted it this time.

The plane shuddered, the vibration reaching me through the axel my shoulders were pressed against. The ocean was still coming closer despite our combined efforts. Snow had begun to fall, the white flakes melting on contact when they reached the churning sea. None of this mattered. We weren't going to make it.

"Please stop this. Both of you," Byte said in my ear, and his too, I presume. "I am begging you. Save your energy for—" her voice cutoff suddenly like the connection had been dropped. "Land. I see land on the radar. We are almost there."

"You can't have her," Toxicwasteman growled. I glanced over, and his eyes were now feral and wild. "She's mine."

I opened my mouth to speak when a sharp pain lanced through my head and I heard a sizzling sound over the wind. I looked up and in the well of the landing gear was another silver alien robot, but it was different. It was the same size, its body a foot across, but it only had four legs, its body wide in the back and tapering into a log proboscis. As I stared, it shot a purple ball out its proboscis and hit me square in the forehead, feeling like I had been struck by a rock, the sizzling sound starting again.

The first robot had sampled me when I was in the engine, the second's legs had turned into this purple goo when I fought it on the wing, now this one was shooting the balls at me.

I couldn't keep holding the plane up and fight this robot. Why did they want to take the plane down?

And then it hit me. They didn't care at all about the plane, whether it landed or not. This was all about finding out more about me, learning better ways to stop and hurt me.

Could there be any doubt the aliens were coming back?

SUMMER 2025, FREDONIA, ARIZONA

THE MINI STORAGE PLACE IN FREDONIA, ARIZONA, WAS NOT much to talk about. Grey cement blocks, cheap metal overhead door. In the metal box she dug up was a wad of cash and a key. She pocketed the cash and used the key to unlock the storage unit. She paused and looked at me in the dimming light. I could see the emotions at play. She was worried, but I didn't think it was the larger how-do-we-survive worry, it was something more personal.

"Listen..." she began, licking her lips, her arms wrapped around her chest despite the warm evening.

This was it. If I wanted it, she would tell me everything. All the plans. All the things she hadn't told me. That look was part worry and part guilt. And I wanted it. I wanted to know everything, and it made me feel good that she wanted to tell me, but... well, it just wasn't the time.

"Let's get safe first," I said, doing my best to give her a relaxed smile, hoping it wasn't one of those crazed, fake, I'm-totally-freaked-out smiles. It wasn't time for that either. "Then we will both have a lot to talk about."

She paused, her eyes searching my face and then she nodded, so I guess my smile wasn't that bad, or the poor dusk lighting explained it—the storage place's lights hadn't gone on yet.

The door rumbled up, puffing out dust to reveal a most atypical storage unit. In other words, there wasn't much in there. In the dim light I could see some cheap metal shelves along one side, some jerry cans, and in the middle of the unit something covered in a sheet that looked just like a—

"No..." I said, a smile blossoming on my face.

"Yup!" The worry and guilt were gone and on her round face was a look of pure joy. Like a kid in the candy store, or like a girl with her motorcycle.

Well, not to say like *any* girl with her motorcycle, but like *this* girl with her motorcycle. Like *my* girl with a motorcycle.

She stepped into the dark space, went to the metal shelves and turned on a battery powered lantern there, which threw out bluish illumination.

Licia pulled the tarp back, dust filling the air, to reveal a Harley-Davidson Sportster 1200. It was a twin cam beauty, long and sleek with two chrome exhaust pipes curling back on the right side, and the tank and the fenders painted an electric blue. It had leather saddle bags and a two-up seat.

It was up on a stand, keeping weight off the tires. It had been properly stored for the long term.

I have flying, I love it and she is terrified by it. She has motorcycles, she loves it and I'm... well, not quite terrified of it, but I don't love it.

Not that there's been much time for motorcycles since we met and all this madness started.

I rode bicycles like a maniac when I was kid, which was my downfall with motorcycles. When I was nineteen, I tried out Robby Holmes's Kawasaki dirt bike and I absolutely loved it. Except the rear brake control was at the foot, not on the handlebar. I was having a great ride through the desert when I had to brake fast for a rabbit, locked the front wheel and went flying.

I broke my right arm and my collar bone. After I recovered, I did ride a little more, just to "get back on the horse," but that early injury spoiled it for me.

From another perspective, though, I do love motorcycles, and that's really about the motor. It's displayed there, all chromed and beautiful. I spent a lot of time working on cars with my father and helped Robby with his motorcycles even after the crash. The Sportster is a particularly beautiful machine.

"The gas has a stabilizer and is about a year old," she said, shaking one of the jerry cans. "You think she'll start up?"

"New oil put in and the gas drained?" I asked.

She nodded.

I checked the exhaust pipes and pulled the rags out—they were put there because rats are notorious for nesting in pipes. I squatted down, looked at the engine, and then looked up at her and the shyness was back on her face. The prep was at least a year old, so there were other people involved in this escape plan. Licia and I had spent the last five years at Casita de Soledad with rare outings and none to this part of Arizona. She had a team that had helped her, and knowing her it was family members. It seemed everywhere we went she had a second cousin or an old friend of her father's.

"Normally," I said with a smile, "the battery would be an issue, but I think we have that covered."

The smile on her face was bright and I realized something. This is what Licia would have wanted back in 2020 if we had gotten the chance to choose. A simple life on the road, just being tourists, just seeing what was around the next bend, the wind ruffling our hair and the scenery whipping by.

The theme from *The Incredible Hulk* played in my head and I imagined Bruce Banner with a gorgeous Harley hitting the road in search of redemption. It didn't quite work, the tune was a bit too sad and a bit too plaintive, but it was a fun idea.

"So..." I began. "The plan is we're riding to the Diane Madison interview. Is it in Los Angeles?"

I knew the answer, but just wanted to see her face.

She shook her head, even in the weird bluish lantern light she suddenly looked younger. "The interview is in New York. We've got to get all the way across the country." She stalked up to me, like she was a big cat after prey, her hand landing on my shoulder, the electric tingle of our energy exchange making me smile. "Won't that be a chore?"

I nodded, not turning around. "A terrible chore. I'll be stuck on that bike behind you, holding on to you for hours a day on that tiny seat."

She ran her finger across my shoulder, her hand resting on my neck, playing with my hair. "Come on, Nik. It'll be fun. We'll make it fun."

And yes, the entire military apparatus of the United States was after us and my wife was flirting with me in a dusty storage unit in Fredonia, Arizona.

I nodded, her tingling hand still on my neck. "I think we should head north first, get out of the area, not take a direct route."

"Cheap hotels along the way," she said, leaning down and whispering in my ear, her breath sweet and warm. "Cash only. Arriving under the cover of darkness. Wine and takeout Chinese food. Back-rubs and doing whatever else we can to relieve the tension of a long ride."

I wanted to turn around and grab her, close the door to the unit, and see what kind of tension could be relieved right here and right now. But after our decades together, I knew what this was. A promise. If I could get the motorcycle working, if I could handle the long days riding on it despite my past trauma and the narrow seat, she would make it well worth my while.

"I like this plan," I said and got to work getting the motorcycle running.

FALL 2006, OVER THE ATLANTIC OCEAN

I was so sick of silver alien morphing robots. I was sick of this 787 and the nor'easter and the struggle to get it back to land. I was tired of the months spent in meetings getting Heroes Incorporated off the ground, negotiating for land for the base, negotiating with the military for autonomy, hiring people, reading contracts. I was even tired of these recruiting trips, trying to convince people that our mission was worthwhile, that banding together was our only chance, that the military wasn't the only way.

And I was so sick of Toxicwasteman and his constant manipulations, his molding of me into what he thought could defeat the aliens and save "his" planet. He wasn't doing this for humanity. He was doing this because aliens invading earth felt personal to his sociopathic brain.

This whole thing felt like a setup. Licia being called away at the last moment so I was alone on the plane. The robots, while clearly alien, showing up time and time again to make this harder, forcing me to find new capabilities. Even this fight for Byte. Was this all a ruse to get me to want Byte more, give her more responsibility, more access? How could I have surprised them with this?

But mostly I was just tired. I had been Neutrinoman—normal, beast mode, or engine—for far too long. I was running on reserves and knew at this point I would be a mess when I became flesh and blood again.

The silver alien robot, clinging to the upper portion of the landing gear, spit another piece of purple goo at me out of its long proboscis. This stuff was purple like the energy weapon that so effectively sapped my power, but it was solid, goopy like jelly. It hit my shoulder and started sizzling, pain spiking through my body.

I pulsed my upper body, just like I had when I tore off the robot's legs on the wing. The pulse worked—it repelled the goo but it also further melted the rubber wheels of the front axle. The robot and I had done this repeatedly, the front two tires were practically gone, and the metal was beginning to pucker and fatigue.

Each of the aft landing gear have two axles with two tires with a large shaft between them. My shoulder was pressed to that central shaft as was Toxicwasteman on the other side. We were a pair. Yellow and green.

"Don't you have a shot?" I yelled at Toxicwasteman.

"No," he shouted back, his voice a growl. "It's up in the well. I can't see it. Don't you have a shot?" We hadn't talked about Byte since this attack started, but the animosity of it lingered.

"Yeah, I have a shot, but you know, holding the plane up, fuel supplies that could ignite. Little problems like that."

I missed being the engine, life was so simple then. I missed beast mode, too, just feeling my way through it.

The robot spit on me again, a spike of pain, the sizzle, and I pulsed it off, feeling my energy wane even further.

I looked at the forward landing gear, but that was the wrong place to apply lift—I'd probably just end up shoving the nose up and destabilizing the plane. I looked over at the starboard engine, the cowling melted back when my reaction had gotten too hot. The alien might be able to follow me there, but at least it would be more exposed.

"Going to the engine," I said as I stopped all the jets, fell away from the landing gear and flew over to the engine. I flew hard up into the forward part of the engine. The exterior metal is just an aerodynamic wrapping around the more complicated interior, but I slammed into it with my upper body fully shielded, making a big dent and resumed my Atlas impression.

The landing gear was behind me, so I couldn't see what the robot might be doing. I was also too far away from Toxicwasteman to shout at him or hear him over the wind and that gave me some small amount of joy.

Below, the ocean was getting choppier, the plane bucking in the wind, the snow getting heavier only to be consumed by the hungry seas. The plane was less than fifty feet above the water and through the grey I couldn't see land yet.

"How far?" I asked quietly. I was talking to Byte.

"Too far," Byte replied.

SUMMER 2025, FREDONIA, ARIZONA

THE THROATY RUMBLE OF A MOTORCYCLE IS A THRILLING thing. I would rather experience that kind of rumble behind the steering wheel of a car, like my father's vintage Dodge Charger, but an engine and a long strip of blacktop is... well, that evening roaring out of Fredonia, Arizona, it sounded like hope.

The vibration of the engine, humming right below us, felt like it was shaking the last few years in Casita de Soledad right off us, dislodging the cramped feeling of being restricted and watched by Homeland Security. The high, scattered clouds hid most of the stars and the dim light turned the rising mesas into dark ghosts on the horizon.

Licia was driving the Sportster and I was perched on the thin seat behind her enjoying her closeness. We had helmets on and well-worn leather jackets with the orange Harley Davidson logo emblazoned on our backs.

"Driving" sounds kind of awkward there, doesn't it? It's usually "riding" when it comes to motorcycles, but that takes away from the skill and precision needed to hurl us down a two-lane road through the desert at night at ninety miles per hour. I was "riding." Licia was "driving."

Licia still had her blond wig on, poking out underneath the helmet, and this made our disguise complete. We weren't two superhero fugitives on the run, we were a couple hitting the road for a long summer adventure.

A couple where the petite woman was the master of the motor-cycle and the man was holding on for dear life. We might get some second looks for that, but no one would suspect that the man was Neutrinoman.

I could feel Licia's tension ease as the miles flew past. We headed north out of Fredonia and were into Utah and through Kanab in no time. This is a scenic route that weaves in between Zion National Park to the west and then Bryce Canyon National Park to the east. The perfect route for summer vacationers in Southern Utah.

There is a simplicity to being on the road. Your life just gets smaller, but in a good way, in the best way. It's about getting to your destination without the load of all the usual possessions and things to do. It's about enjoying the journey and seeing new things. And for us, it was about a lot more than that. It was about our future and our survival. And that was there, but back in the background. The rumble of the motor and the hum of the tires on the pavement eased all of that away.

Soon the desert gave way as we climbed, sagebrush and pinon trees flickering by in the headlight of the Harley. We zipped past Mount Carmel Junction and through several other tiny little blips of civilization as the road continued to rise and we started to see pine trees instead of pinons.

The night was warm, in the lower sixties, and the wind felt good. We soon climbed all the way into the pine trees, the land-scape looking very similar to Flagstaff. We were cutting through a corner of Dixie National Forest, dirt forest service roads diving off here and there. Our plan was to drive all night, get well clear of the area, before finding some takeout Chinese food, some wine, and a cheap hotel.

We zipped past an RV just off one of the Forest Service roads. The RV's headlights were on and I caught a glimpse of some sharp movement from behind it. It was one of the smaller type RVs, built on a van frame. It was only a glimpse, the bright lights hitting my eyes as we flashed by.

It took a few breaths as my mind tried to piece the shadows together, tried to make sense of the blur of motion.

"Turn around!" I shouted, my heart thumping hard.

"What? Why?" Licia asked.

"That was the Polar Express," I said, and I could feel her shoulders rise and fall in a "that's nice, but we're trying to escape here."

"I think they're in trouble," I added, my heart pounding harder. In that glimpse, I had seen four people and the way they moved wasn't right. Someone's hand was reaching out and someone else was throwing themselves towards them.

It could be nothing, just my imagination, fueled by recent experience. But Jean and Alan had been such a nice couple. If we kept on going, I would always wonder.

I didn't need to say anything else. Licia turned so fast I had to hold tight to her waist and soon we were roaring back towards them, the growl of the Harley taking on a more urgent tone.

FALL 2006, OVER THE ATLANTIC OCEAN

THE TERM "LAND" AS A NOUN REFERS TO TERRA FIRMA, BUT AS a verb it's about something coming down from the air onto the ground. But what do you call it when something is coming down from the ground onto the water? That can't be landing, and "water landing" just sounds stupid if you think about it. Maybe water should be used as a verb. As in the 787 airplane Toxicwasteman and I were trying to keep in the air was about to water onto the ocean.

No, that sounds stupid too, if descriptive.

Chop from the stormy ocean was close enough now that it was splashing the underside of the fuselage, sloshing into my neutrino jets and turning to steam. The view from this elevation was so very different. From up high, the seas had been a churning, but undifferentiated, mass. As we descended, the waves resolved into individual features, and now I could see the swells were ten feet tall, some larger, the space between the top of the waves and me less than twelve feet.

"Five thousand meters," Byte said in my ear. She had been

counting off the distance for a while. And not the distance to JFK, but the distance to Jones Beach State Park on the outer edge of Long Island. The plan—if you can call it that—was to beach the plane there.

Hey, "beach" works fine as a verb, but water sure doesn't. Bad for the plane, bad for the English language.

Except we couldn't keep the plane aloft that long. It just wasn't going to happen. And a few thousand meters from shore in this weather would be as bad as a few hundred miles.

"Come on, Boy Scout," Toxicwasteman said in my ear. "I know that's not all you got. Come on! Remember my promise. I'll turn myself in. I swear to god that I will turn myself in. I've never lied to you."

And he hadn't lied, that I know of, but that didn't mean that I believed him. It was the "swear to god" part that ruined it for me. You could almost hear the lowercase "g" when he said "god." I was pretty sure he didn't believe in a power higher than himself. But the time to fight over Byte or anything else was past. For me, talking was pretty much past. Every ounce of energy I could come up with was in service of staying in my Neutrino form and keeping the airplane in the air.

I wanted to shoot something pithy back like, "Great. You turn yourself in and Byte will be free to come work for me." But I didn't have the energy for it and I didn't want to destabilize him enough so he stopped doing his part over on the landing gear.

The metal of the engine groaned as I thrust harder, the wing creaking, and I was worried that it might snap off. A wing is designed to hold the plane up, but with the lift of the flowing air applied across the entire surface of the wing, not me and my Atlas impression at the engine.

I don't know if you've ever noticed it, but wings have quite a bit of flex. I've seen it plenty of times on the runway, planes taxiing and the wings flexing in ways that are a bit disconcerting.

Wings are not designed for this kind of concentrated force.

"Four thousand meters," Byte's computerized voice said in my head.

I glanced ahead, but I could not see any land, only the grey sky and the grey ocean through the steam.

My mind drifted to Licia as I worried that I wouldn't be able to hold onto my neutrino form long enough, that I would be lost in the ocean below before the plane, that I wouldn't get to see her again.

And how was I to defend the human race from an alien attack when a couple of stupid robots had made saving this plane nearly impossible? Even with all the new tricks I discovered. There was at least one robot still onboard, it hadn't followed me from the landing gear, which was good. I didn't think I could withstand another attack.

"Three thousand meters."

Was that a slash of brown on the horizon? Was land finally in sight?

Endurance running was part of the training the military had me do. Learning how to push when it seemed there was nothing left and then pushing some more. I missed those early days when I had less freedom, yes, but a lot less responsibility. I didn't have to recruit or make hiring decisions or worry that each choice I made would be the mistake that would lead to humanity's disaster.

But humanity was a disaster already. The microcosm of Toxicwasteman and I fighting over Byte without her saying more than a few words about it. The cliché of powerful men fighting over the limited resources that is this particular woman. Misogyny. Attachment. Ego.

And that was just this one little battle. Humanity was battling all the time. Genocide. War. Murder. Violence. Not to mention the ugly blood sport of politics.

Maybe the aliens are right about us. Maybe we should be eliminated for the good of all.

The waves were now cresting just below my feet, the low elevation and the rising steam destroying my visibility of anything but the angry ocean.

"Two thousand meters."

Byte wasn't even offering encouragement anymore. Just stating the facts. As if she was exhausted with this fight. The fight for survival, the fight for her.

And while humanity was a mess, there was Licia, my own representative of what was right in this world. Love. Intimacy. Caring for someone else more than you care for yourself.

And did Toxicwasteman, the villain and sociopath, care for Byte more than he cared for himself? Or was she just a possession he was attached to, something he "owned"?

My mind raged as I struggled to keep the plane from the water, struggled to keep my form and then—

The waves receded and weren't peaking just below my feet, the steam dissipating and I could see land ahead and I could also see... Well I couldn't believe what I was seeing.

The nor'easter choppy sea was calming and quickly. The wind hadn't stopped, the snow was still falling, but a strip of ocean right below the plane and running to the beach became significantly calmer. The wind was still whipping at it, but the waves receded and that strip of calm water looked eerily like a runway welcoming us back to land.

This wasn't natural. This wasn't possible.

What the hell?

SUMMER 2025, SOUTHERN UTAH

LICIA WASN'T HOLDING BACK AS SHE DROVE US BACK TOWARD
the Polar Express. She was hunched down and going fast. I leaned
down too and held on tight.

The whine of the engine told me she was pushing it hard and I
had this terrible thought. What if I hadn't seen anything at all in
the flash of light as we passed the RV? What if it wasn't even Jean
and Alan and the Polar Express? What if my paranoid mind had
made all of this up for reasons that would take years of therapy to
understand?

My stomach was tight from those thoughts and the adrenaline
of the ride.

"Two men with them," Licia shouted as the RV first came into
sight and I couldn't distinguish any individuals, but she could with
that raven enhanced sight of hers. "I can't tell if they are harmed.
Jean and Alan look terrified."

More adrenaline dumped into my bloodstream. What I wanted
to do was change into Neutrinoman and fly to the rescue. But that

wouldn't be a good idea. First of all, we were on the run from the entire US government, and secondly, I didn't have a spare set of clothing.

That last one, admittedly, sounds a bit shallow, and it is. But time after time I've been in the strangest of circumstances without any clothing. That kind of thing can really worm into your psyche.

"Valentine," Licia shouted. Thoughts of not using powers must have been running through her head too.

Valentine Oscar, the man who served as my... God, what do I call him? He was part bodyguard, part confidant, part moral compass. I know I haven't written much about him yet—we're not to that part of the story—but trust me when I say that the utterance of his name made me feel even more than what I had already been feeling.

Many didn't survive the war and I've been careful not to share too much, but Valentine is one of those and that is all I can say right now.

Right then, Licia was saying "Valentine" because it was the easiest way to convey that we would have to do this battle as mortals. Valentine's mission was to keep us safe and part of that was training us in hand-to-hand combat.

Licia drove at top speed, like we were going to pass the RV by. It was parked right off the pavement just down the dirt forest service road. But she braked hard, the rubber squealing against the pavement, and then the hard-packed dirt as she took us off the road and brought us to a stop on the other side of the RV in a cloud of dust.

We didn't talk. She put the kickstand down and went towards the front of the RV as I went towards the back, keeping my steps soft, my center of gravity low. I took my helmet off, but kept ahold of it thinking it might be useful as a weapon.

The truth here was that I wasn't needed. Licia could handle this, being able to use her powers in a limited and non-lethal way without transformation. Like in Fredonia when she had charged the battery just by touching it.

By saying "Valentine" she had been telling me that she was going to try to not use her powers. We were undercover, after all.

I sneaked around the back of the RV and paused. I could smell sweat, unwashed bodies, cigarettes, and overcooked meat. I could hear the rustling of clothing and boots shifting on the dirt, and a man whispering, "One word, Pops, and she dies."

More adrenaline, a righteous fury fueling me, waking me up, making me feel alive. This was worse for Jean and Alan than I had thought, making it a fight worth having. A plan clicked together in my mind, one that I couldn't tell Licia about, but hoped she would follow my lead.

"Not tonight," I said loudly as I stepped out from the back of the RV.

There was a small folding table set up in front of the RV, on it was a lantern and a propane stove with two overcooked hamburgers.

Jean and Alan were there, tracks of dried tears on Jean's wrinkled face, Alan's shoulders stooped and his back bent. They looked much older than when we had met earlier that day. Fear was written on their faces, but also confusion. The look one gets when the world suddenly turns and it isn't quite what you thought it was. I've had that look on my face many times.

There were two men with them. The one had Jean's hair in his fist and held a 9mm to the base of her head as he pressed her against the door of the RV.

The other man had his gun pointed at my head and slowly pulled back the hammer. "You don't want to do this," he said. He was tall and thin with stringy brown hair down to his shoulders, the lantern light making his face seem downright cadaverous. Alan was sitting in a chair next to him, the man's hand on Alan's shoulder.

The one with Jean was shorter and plumper but had a

hollowed-out look on his face that made me think they were in withdrawal.

Twenty years ago, drug use went up considerably when the alien threat came to life. People acted differently, some turned to God, some turned to the bottle or drugs, some pretended it wasn't happening, and some fought. That trend lingers today as the world tries to put the trauma of the war behind us.

These two looked like tweekers, desperate for the next hit of crack or meth or speed. The forest is not a usual hangout for them, just bad luck for Jean and Alan.

"Oh, I think I do," I said with a smile. "Jean, Alan, you guys all right?" If these tweekers had any brain cells left, I wanted them to know that I knew these people and wouldn't be leaving.

"We most definitely are not," Alan said, his voice shaking and barely above a whisper.

My plan, as most of my plans are, was quite simple. Keep the men distracted while Licia takes them out. If I kept all eyes on me, she would feel free to use her powers and to draw electricity from these boys until they passed out like those buffalo at Yellowstone.

"I think we can work this out," I said slowly. "We've got a bike. A nice one. A Harley. How about I give you a hundred bucks and the bike and you let these folks go?"

Tweeker two's eyes flicked from me to the RV, towards the bike on the other side. He licked his lips. "Let me see the money."

I nodded and slowly reached into my front pocket. Licia had given me some of our cash reserves. I could hear her moving, her footsteps faint on the dirt, too quiet for them to hear. I pulled out a sizable wad of cash and both of their eyes lit up. I had their full attention.

I slowly pulled one and then two hundred-dollar bills out. "Let's make it two hundred. I'm feeling generous." I gestured with the money and their eyes were following it like I was holding a fresh soup bone in front of a hungry dog.

"Now," I began, hoping that would signal Licia as I stepped closer waving the money around even more, "I'm sure we can—"

Licia stepped into view, lightning arced from their bodies to Licia's outstretched hands and they both went down with a thud.

So much for hand-to-hand combat. So much for our cover.

FALL 2006, OVER THE ATLANTIC OCEAN

THE STORMY OCEAN WAS CALMING, BUT JUST BELOW THE LOW-flying 787 and extending like a runway to the beach. The waves shrank, until it was only the wind frothing up the water at the surface. Beyond the runway of water, the ocean was a chaotic mess with twelve-foot swells.

I was imagining it. That had to be the explanation. The only place you hear about water doing something like this was in the Bible where Moses parted the Red Sea.

"What the hell?" I mumbled.

"I'm not doing that," I heard Toxicwasteman say in my ear. "Neutrino, are you doing that?"

So I wasn't imagining it. I craned my neck around looking for the reflective silver of an alien robot, thinking maybe I wasn't imagining this and it was the next challenge the alien robots were setting for me.

But no robots.

"I'm not doing that," I replied.

"Well, then who the hell is?"

And then the water runway began to rise, closing the six feet that remained between the plane and the ocean as if it was reaching out for the plane.

I looked around for robots again, scanned what I could see of the skies for alien ships. What kind of power would it take to move this much water? It wasn't human, that was for sure.

"Don't worry. It's okay," Byte's perfectly calm computerized voice said in my ear.

"Don't worry?" Toxicwasteman shouted. "Are you out of you mind? What do you mean don't worry? There's a goddamn runway made out of water below us."

"Yes," Byte continued. "I know. I need the two of you to cease your lifting activities and move to the front of the plane in ten seconds. You will need to slow it for the landing."

I was as confused as Toxicwasteman, who continued to ask Byte questions which were not answered, but I didn't have any questions of my own. I stared at the dark water and felt... well, it was clearly a runway after all, it was reaching for the plane, the beach was getting closer.

As the plane continued to fall and the ocean grew closer, Toxicwasteman's queries became louder.

"Five. Four," Byte said, ignoring him, her computerized voice completely calm. He didn't seem to be enjoying this. I didn't know if this was all part of their act, but he sure didn't seem to know what was going on.

"Really, Byte?" he said. "You're going to ignore me. You're going to act like this is all normal to you. Well, I'll tell you one thing. This is *not* normal!"

It wasn't lost on me, even in the chaos of the situation, that he was calling her Byte not Gayle. Was this from habit or was it because Gayle wasn't her name?

"Three."

The water runway had risen and the plane had fallen, the calm water rising above Toxicwasteman's feet. He was lower than me, still on the landing gear, his green thrust producing so much steam I couldn't see him.

"Two."

I caught a flash of something moving rapidly in the water. Was it a dolphin or a pod of dolphins?

"One."

I gladly stopped my Atlas impression and flew right above the water to the front of the plane. Through the cockpit window, I could see the captain, a look of terror on her face as she stared down at the water. However Byte was coordinating this, it was clear she hadn't involved them. I guess she had taken the plane over.

Toxicwasteman and I arrived at the front of the plane at the same time, his green face forming the most sour expression.

"Welcome to my world," I shouted cheerfully. I wanted to make sure he heard me over the wind in case Byte wasn't patching our voices through our earbuds anymore. I think Toxicwasteman had spent most of this time thinking he was in charge and he had just discovered that his partner and mate had a lot going on that he didn't know about.

"Shut it!" he growled.

The landing gear retracted into the fuselage and the flaps on the wings went down a bit as the plane gently touched the water with a splash and then bounced back into the air like a rock skipping on calm water.

My fatigue forgotten, I flew ahead a bit for a better view and watched as the water reached up even farther and embraced the plane, this water runway rising well above the swells of the nor'easter beyond it.

Intelligence was guiding this, an intelligence that Byte was not afraid of and knew something about. I was all smiles as I flew and watched, Toxicwasteman barking out obscenities.

The wave or water runway or whatever it was effectively caught the plane and slowly lowered it as the beach approached.

When we were a few football fields out, Byte said in my ear, "Position yourself at the nose of the plane and slow it. Now."

I twisted around in the air and slammed into the nose of the plane, metal crunching beneath me, my shoulders shielded. Toxicwasteman did the same far enough away so we didn't touch—our quantum forms don't mix will.

We both thrusted, my yellow neutrino jets mixing with his green jets and black smoke.

Jones Beach State Park sits off of Long Island right on the Atlantic and is one of the most popular beaches in the New York area. It's got a wide sandy beach, broad parking lots and roads, and the Theodore Roosevelt Nature Center. But it's not a very wide piece of land and the plane needed to be stopped.

Byte spoke continuously. Counting off our distance from the land, telling us to increase or decrease our efforts. Too much and the plane wouldn't make it, too little and we'd plow through the sand and scrape along the parking lots or crash through buildings.

At the end, as the water became shallow and the beach approached, it was... well, I couldn't see it clearly from my vantage, and no one was out in this weather with a camera, but picture a 787 airplane, all two hundred feet of it, surfing on an incoming wave with the wind whipping and the snow pelting down.

The "water runway" effect went away for those last few yards, the raised water crashing like any other wave. The noise of the 787 smashing into the beach was deafening. The sand flying up, the sound of crunching metal loud against the background din of the storm, the plane bucking and groaning, the screams of the passengers barely audible against it all.

Toxicwasteman was bucked off the nose, but I held my position.

"More," Byte said. "We need more."

I thrust with all my might, adding my yell to the din of noise as the plane scraped over the sand.

We were positioned perfectly. The West End parking lot had a huge tongue of sand extending from it to the beach and the plane slid off the water-soaked sand near the ocean to the dry sand behind and onto the wide tongue of sand leading to the parking lot.

Byte had aimed well. This trajectory was about as safe as it could be for a 787 landing on the beach.

I screamed and thrust and gave it all I could, the crunching noise of the metal of the plane bending further against my force, effectively burying my face and shoulders in the metal.

It wasn't enough to get the plane to dry land, it had to be stopped before it took too much damage. Toxicwasteman had been thrown off, it was just me. I had to do it. I had to stop it. Fatigue didn't matter. Aliens and their robots didn't matter. Heroes Incorporated didn't matter.

The front part of me buried in the plane, I switched into a more elemental state. I wasn't quite the engine, but the need drove me to something primal, something more elemental.

My screams of exertion melted into the roar of my effort. My plane. I must stop it. I must succeed.

Time slipped away from me and I gladly fell into the single-minded purpose of stopping the plane.

"... is enough, Nik. You did it. You stopped us. Nik. Please. Stop."

Byte's words came to me as if from a dream and I returned to myself and stopped thrusting, pushing myself back out of the cratered front of the plane.

I felt my deep fatigue again, barely holding onto my neutrino form. I fell to the sand, turning to flesh and blood halfway down and landing hard, the wind icy cold, snow falling on my bare skin.

But there it was, the 787 after its beach landing sitting right in front of the snow-covered parking lot.

I laughed, a manic, high-pitched sound, and then the cold truly reached me and I began to shiver.

I could hear sirens in the distance—help was on the way.

Which was good. I would freeze in no time out here.

I was stumbling around naked over the cold, snow-covered sand, snow sticking to my hair, my teeth chattering, the wind howling as I gawked at the 787.

The nose was pushed in, a crater about four feet deep... I hoped the crew got out of the cockpit in time. The path the plane had carved in the sand extended beyond the nose. In my mania to stop it, I had pushed the plane backwards and I was paying the price.

Besides the chattering teeth, my head spiked with pain and my gut was sucked in. I think I had lost five or ten pounds of muscle. This is how it works. During my reaction, the nonessential me will be consumed—including much of the bacterial colonies in my gut, leading to all kinds of fun in the bathroom later on. And, I was learning that if I kept pushing, if my will held, the reaction would start to consume more essential parts of me, like fat and then muscle.

Before the transformation, I was well-hydrated and healthy. After this long one, I was dehydrated and looked like I had been very ill for a long time.

I heard voices inside the plane and the sirens were getting closer.

"You can't have her," Tom Tyree said as he strode across the sand naked. He was much taller than me, his shoulders back as he marched across the snowy sand. He was gaunter than usual. He had been transformed for a long time too, and it must have taken its toll on him.

"Sh... Shut up, Tom," I said, my teeth chattering, my arms hugging my bare chest.

"You ca... can't have her," he repeated, walking boldly towards me like it was a sunny day on a nude beach even though his teeth were chattering too.

Tom never cared about his nudity. If there is one thing I could take from him, that would be it. Not his endless confidence, there's something wrong with you if you think you are always right. Not his complete lack of morals in pursuing his goals. I would just like to not be worried about being naked.

"I ddd... don't want to possess her," I said. "I want her to work for mmm... me."

"No!" he yelled as he reached me, his chest puffed out, his green eyes fierce.

And then it dawned on me. The emergency was over and he hadn't fled. Was he really going to turn himself in?

"Why nnn... not?" I yelled back.

"She's mine!"

"You keep saying that, but what the hell do you mmm... mean by it?" Part of me knew I should be paying attention to the plane, worried about my own survival, but there in front of the beached 787, I just kind of lost it. I was dehydrated and starving and freezing, my head pounding. I had been through way too much and I was just over him.

"Can you tell mmm... me that?" I yelled. "Are you saying that you own her? That you control her every action? That you make her every decision? Are you saying that she is your property, Tom, because I really hope that is not what you are saying."

"She's mmm... mine," he said quieter, his eyes flicking from me down to the sand, his thin shoulders slumping.

"You've nnn... never needed anyone before, have you?" I asked, my voice back to a normal tone, loud enough for him to hear me over the wind. Behind me I could hear sounds coming from the plane but I didn't pay attention. This seemed important.

He hugged his chest and shook his head, still not looking at me.

"And you nnn... need her."

He nodded.

Tom Tyree was like a child when it came to this. He didn't know how to act. But that doesn't mean I was going to teach him.

"And none of that matters when the aliens come bbb... back and we aren't strong enough to sss... stop them," I said.

He looked up, his wolfish grin appearing briefly but then melting away. "You said *when* nnn... not *if*."

I did. The damn robots had pushed me over the edge and I couldn't really hope that the Arcturian Alliance would somehow find humanity worthy of preservation. There were plenty of days when I doubted it myself.

"And that is why I need her to be part of Heroes Incorporated, which was *your* ddd... damn idea anyway."

He bit his lip and shook his head. "Nnn... no. *Her* idea." He nodded back at the plane and I turned around and saw that they had opened the hatch. A woman with long dark hair was the first to slide down the orange emergency slice.

It was Byte still in her wig, her hands full of blankets and she ran towards us over the snow and the sand.

I had forgotten about the earbuds. She had heard everything we had said. I remembered when she had told me that Tom Tyree had found her after her transformation, when she didn't understand what had happened to her. She told me how he had saved her.

Maybe she was the one saving him now.

"Here," she said, handing us both three of those thin airline blankets. It wasn't much, but at least it helped.

"Www... will you work for Heroes Incorporated?" I asked. I wasn't going to let it go.

She nodded away from the plane and walked swiftly towards the ocean. Tom and I shared a puzzled look and I began to wonder who had been in charge of LoVE all this time. Was it the psychopathic Tom Tyree or the clever Byte whose real name may or may not be Gayle?

We followed her down to the beach, the ocean roaring as huge waves crashed onto the sand, all signs of the water runway gone.

"Of course," she said with a wan smile before turning to Tom. "And I will keep working for LoVE."

I nodded, a stupid smile on my face feeling in that moment that I had won some kind of victory, but had I?

She turned to me. "My identity must remain secret. Do you understand?"

I nodded. Behind us I could see that a growing group of passengers had slid down the orange slide and the emergency crews had just reached the parking lot.

She took a step towards Tom, rose onto her toes, and kissed him on the cheek. "Now, neither of you follow me. Okay?"

We both nodded and then she walked into the ocean. When the wild waves had reached her calves she turned back. "Seriously. Don't follow me."

I just stared. What the hell was going on?

A huge wave, like some giant hand, rose up from the ocean, twice as tall as any previous waves. It crashed over her and then she was gone.

SUMMER 2025, SOUTHERN UTAH

ALAN HADN'T SEEN A THING, BOTH THE TWEEKERS HAVING been behind him, but a look of recognition was blossoming in Jean's face as she stared at Licia.

I was using some duct tape and binding both the tweekers at their hands and feet.

Licia had grabbed one of the guns quickly, waved it around briefly, and told Alan it was a tranquilizer gun. He was in shock and was so glad to be alive he would have bought anything, could dismiss the sizzling sound of the lightning as something he imagined, could ignore the sharp scent of ozone that still lingered in the air.

Jean, on the other hand, had seen that lightning, at least out of the corner of her eye.

"What now?" Alan asked. He was wandering around the fold-up table, his path erratic as he kept mumbling "Oh, my." I felt for the guy, this was not normal, not the kind of thing you can—or should—plan for.

And "what now" was the question of the hour.

"Take a moment," Licia said, calmly going over to Alan and putting her hand on his shoulder and guiding him towards his wife. Jean's eyebrow arched and she watched them like a hawk. "Just take a moment. Get your feet underneath you and then you guys can get back on the road."

They had parked right off the road, not in the kind of place you would camp in. You'd go farther down the dirt road, find a secluded spot. It looks like they had just stopped for a meal.

"What about them?" Jean asked, her tone a half an octave higher than normal.

"We'll take care of them," I said.

Her eyes widened as she looked more closely at me, her mouth forming an "O," another look of recognition on her face.

Except for my books, the world hadn't thought much about us or seen us for years. With the Quantum Accords of 2020 we were shipped out to the desert, the lawsuits against us settled, as the world tried desperately to forget what had happened and get back to normal.

There had been a lot of shouting and a lot of blaming after the war. Us surviving q-morphs didn't end up on the right side of all of that. Jean's recognition was quickly turning into distrust.

"How did you find us?" she asked quietly, her arms around her husband protectively.

I shrugged. "Just luck. I noticed the Polar Express as we rode by and something just didn't look right."

"And what a piece of luck that," Alan said. "You guys... you saved us. Jean, Lee and Neil just saved us."

I was glad he mentioned the names Licia had made up for us when they picked us up near Jacob Lake. I had forgotten them.

"After you guys are on your way, we'll call the cops and take care of them," Licia said with a smile. "No need to ruin your vacation."

Alan nodded enthusiastically, but Jean shook her head. She probably thought we would do something horrible to them.

"I think they'll want our statement," Jean said slowly.

Licia shrugged. "Okay, then." She turned to me. "You done? Are they secure?"

I had them leaning up against the back tire of the RV. Their wrists were taped together behind their backs and their ankles were taped together. I had checked their pulses, and they were fine. They would have a hell of a headache on top of their withdrawal symptoms when they woke up, but they would live. "Yup. Secure."

I had also searched their pockets and found a sock stuffed with jewelry and Alan's wallet which I had returned. It was a simple robbery. I'm guessing if we hadn't come by, they would have stolen the RV.

"Good," Licia said with a nod. "We'll be going then. We've got a long way to go yet tonight. Good luck, you guys." She said it sweetly, but it was clear she had seen Jean's looks. We couldn't stay until the cops came.

Alan protested, wanted to thank us, made Licia write their cell phone down and insisted that we call them if they could ever help us. Jean was restrained, but thanked us too.

Soon we were back on the road, Licia driving the Harley even faster. We had no idea when Jean was going to tell the authorities about us, but it was pretty clear she would.

I felt a little bit like Bruce Banner hitting the road once again. We had done the *right* thing, of that I had no doubt, but it clearly wasn't the best thing for us.

39 / OCEAN ANOMALIES

FALL 2006, JONES BEACH STATE PARK, NEW YORK

THE OCEAN DOESN'T ACT THIS WAY. IT DOESN'T CALM AND form a runway in the middle of a nor'easter. Rogue, handlike waves don't rise up and snatch people off the beach right after they tell you not to follow them.

I rushed towards the ocean, my bare feet on the wet sand where Byte had just been.

"Don't bother," Tom growled from behind me.

I turned. "Ddd... didn't you see what hhh... happened?"

He rolled his eyes and sighed. "She knows what she's doing. Believe me, Neutrino, she knows what she's doing."

My teeth chattering, I babbled on about the ocean and the weird waves and he just sighed and rolled his eyes again. "Byte is fff... fine," he finally said, turning and looking back at the plane. The beach was flooded with people, with flashing lights in the parking lot beyond. Police, paramedics, and firefighters were there, escorting people away.

"Excuse me," he said slowly, looking at the scene, "but I've got to go keep my promise."

"What?" I asked. "You're really going to turn yourself in?"

He turned back to me, his wolfish grin back and a sparkle in his eyes. "I told you, Neutrino, I've never lied to you and I will always keep my word. You got the plane back. Byte is safe. I'm turning myself in now, and I'll give you all the credit."

I just stared as Tom wandered back towards the plane. "I am Tom Tyree," he shouted, his voice rising above the storm, "the q-morph known as Toxic, and even though I just helped save the lives of every person on this plane, I am turning myself in."

He raised his hands, the blankets falling from his tall, gaunt body, and there were gasps. Several police officers were on him in seconds and had him on the ground and were cuffing him. He turned and looked back at me after they got him standing again. His green eyes drilled into mine and he nodded once before they hauled him away.

It was a brief, dramatic scene, just what you would expect from him. And it felt like a scene, part of a play, something designed with a specific outcome in mind. Tom's stated objective was clear: defeating the aliens, saving the world, and using me to do that. How the hell did Byte getting swallowed by the ocean and Tom getting led off in cuffs accomplish that?

A young police officer jogged down to me. "How did you do it, Mr. Nichols?" she asked breathlessly, handing me a winter parka which I gratefully pulled on over the blankets. "How did you get him to come in peacefully?"

I shook my head. "No idea."

She looked puzzled. "We should go, sir, the storm is only going to get worse."

I nodded, my gaze being drawn back to the ocean. "Can you give me a minute?"

She smiled, it was one of those star-struck smiles, and I hated it. I didn't want to be looked up to like that. I had powers, yes, but I was as insecure as the next human and was faking it just like the rest of us. She jogged back to the plane and I took a step farther into the water, the waves reaching my calves as they hungrily licked the beach.

The ocean was a churning mess. What had happened? What was going on?

I saw the wave form, out about fifty yards, the chaotic chop coming together and forming a bigger wave right in front of me, the same kind of wave that had taken Byte.

I sighed. I was so tired, swaying as the wind buffeted me. The roar of the ocean was soothing and I didn't move, not one bit. Not when the water receded as the wave approached, not when it rose up like a giant hand, and not when it crashed down and pulled me into the cold, churning ocean.

THE HARLEY SPORTSTER HURLED DOWN THE TWO-LANE blacktop of Utah Route 12, the headlight stabbing out and revealing juniper and pine trees growing from salmon-colored soil. We were near Bryce Canyon National Park, having headed east as soon as we could instead of going north on 89.

If I thought Licia had driven fast before, I was wrong. The motorcycle's engine howled and the miles whipped past. We had to assume that Jean had told the police about us, that the net was closing in.

And if she did and if it was, going faster probably didn't matter much. There just weren't that many roads in this part of Utah. It wouldn't be hard to watch for a couple on a Harley on all of them.

Her back was tense as we whipped around a corner, dove into the left lane and passed a pickup driving at a sane speed, and then zagged back into the right lane.

It's gorgeous country we were driving through, forests and deserts in shades ranging from taupe to ochre, mesas and canyons everywhere. Some of the most beautiful land in the country. I wished we really were tourists taking our time during the day, stopping to see the sights, staying at the kind of funky old motels you can find in the little towns that are sprinkled around out here.

"I love you," I shouted loud enough so she could hear me.

It's what I say when I have to say something and I have no idea what it should be. I say it because it's true. I say it because it is something that should be said, but still it feels empty sometimes.

"I love you, too," she shouted back. And I knew she did, but there were no assurances added that we would figure this out, that we would make it, that everything would be okay.

Everything wasn't okay, and we had no idea if we would make it.

I appreciate that about her and about our relationship. I don't want assurances that aren't based in reality. I would have loved it right then, believe me, a kind lie to soothe my worry, but we didn't do it that way, so we declared our love and kept going.

What else could we do?

The guilt tried to creep back in as the wind whipped by. Guilt over what just happened at Casita de Soledad, but other guilt, older guilt—a war can leave you with a lifetime of things to second-guess.

Maybe if the war hadn't gotten so messy, maybe we could have had a normal life in 2020 instead of our isolated desert home. No drowning in lawsuits. No Quantum Metamorph Accord. No Project Vulcan. No constant surveillance. No running for our lives through this beautiful land instead of being tourists.

And that's the thing about guilt, you let a little in and it brings all the other guilts with it.

Without thinking about it, I sat up a little, pulling away from Licia a bit.

"Don't!" she shouted as we pulled out of a tight turn.

She was referring to my shift in position. We were going so fast that changing the bike's center of gravity was dangerous. But she might have been talking about where my head had gone. She knows exactly what my lame "I love you" meant.

I leaned forward into her and gave her a tiny squeeze, just enough for her to feel it. Another way to say "I love you."

I pushed back the guilt and tried to think. We had to get to the interview with Diane Madison in New York. We had to plead our case in public, reveal how we had been treated, hope that it would go our way.

But if Jean said anything, we would end up in an untenable encounter with the police or, worse yet, the military. And this was something we couldn't plan for—not really much more than we turn into our q-morph forms and I fly us out of here.

As I worried and pondered, we roared through the Grand Staircase-Escalante National Monument, turned on Route 24 and went past Capitol Reef National Park and down into the Utah desert.

It was still dark when we made it to I-70, the gas tank low and our exhaustion high. We were about 250 miles away from where we left Jean and Alan. Licia pulled us to the side of the road right before the on-ramp, the lights of the cars cutting through the night.

This is dry desert with lumpy hills and mesas in tan to reddish tones, all of them like hulking ghosts in the dark.

"Maybe she didn't say anything," I offered, referring to Jean. It had been hours and no signs of military helicopters or one police car.

Licia shrugged.

"We should rest," I added.

She shrugged again.

"And eat." My stomach was a tight knot and my head was light. You really want to be in good shape physically before transforming. I was still vibrating from all the miles and my butt really hurt from being perched on the narrow seat.

When the silence stretched out, I said the other stand-in phrase, the one that was not nearly as positive as the "I love you" one. "I'm sorry," I whispered.

"Me too," she said, not turning, still looking at the highway.

And that's really the worst response. "I love you" echoed back can build you up. "I'm sorry" coming back does the opposite.

And as much as my ego wanted to take it all on, make it all about me, my rational mind fought back. I wasn't responsible for the cosmic waves or the accident at Palo Verde Nuclear Generating Station that changed me. I didn't make the aliens try to eradicate us. I didn't make the military do all the stupid things they did. I didn't plant Project Vulcan underneath us. I wasn't the only one that fought the war.

But this, today, sure felt like it was all my fault. First with blowing up the bomb under us at Casita de Soledad and then having us turn around and help Jean and Alan.

And that's the thing about ego and guilt. I think the ego feeds off of it, because even though it sucks, it is all about you. That previous statement assumes that Licia didn't have any say in either blowing up Project Vulcan or helping Jean and Alan, which of course she did.

"Let's risk a stop," I said gently. "We need food and rest."

She nodded, not turning around. "Next town, then."

We got on I-70, the traffic almost nonexistent this early in the morning, and headed east into the unknown.

FALL 2006, THE ATLANTIC OCEAN

THE OCEAN TOOK ME, AND I DIDN'T FIGHT. PARTIALLY because I was beyond exhausted, partially because I didn't want to face crowds or reporters or police, and partially because I knew something was going on and I wanted to understand it.

How much energy does it take to create a runway of smooth water in the middle of a nor'easter? What kind of intelligence would have to be behind that?

Well... there would have to be a high level of intelligence and a massive amount of energy. It's the latter that was driving me to distraction. What could possibly have enough power to control the ocean like that?

It didn't hurt when the wave crashed into me. In fact, I didn't feel wet... well, any wetter than I already was from the snow that had been falling.

My eyes were shut and I felt intense pressure and my empty stomach lurched like I was on a high-g amusement park ride. I held my breath and heard the sound of water all around me. It wasn't like the white noise of crashing waves or the slosh of water in a bathtub, it was more than that and subtler at the same time. It was a lot like those sounds compressed and happening very fast all at once.

I was moving. The water was moving.

I kept my limbs close and didn't move my body and it almost felt like something huge and amorphous was carrying me.

As the seconds ticked by, my lungs began to burn and I heard a voice that came out of all those water sounds. It was distant, but close, strangely musical. "Breathe..." it whispered.

I exhaled and carefully sipped air in through my mouth and... no water. There was air around me and I began breathing again, the sense of motion accelerating.

I slowly opened my eyes and saw... amorphous grey, almost black. I couldn't make out anything, but the grey wasn't still, it was moving like when you squeeze your eyes shut tight and see unnamable patterns in the dark. This was like that but soot gray, not pitch black.

Seeing the movement increased my sense of vertigo and I squeezed my eyes back shut. Whatever this thing was, this power and intelligence, it had me and it didn't feel like it was going to let me go anytime soon.

42 / GREEN RIVER

THE NEXT TOWN, AS IT TURNS OUT, WAS ONLY A FEW MILES down I-70. Green River, Utah. It's just a blip in the road with a population of less than a thousand, one of those forgettable southwest desert towns except for one thing. It sits on the Green River as it flows lazily towards the Colorado River.

It felt perfect to me. Just the kind of stop we needed.

We pulled into a truck stop right off the highway, gassed up and walked into the restaurant, a greasy-spoon style diner that had my stomach jumping for joy. Not that exciting for Licia, her being a vegetarian and much more health conscious than me.

It felt strange not to have the rumbling Harley beneath me, and the world seemed to be moving even when I was still. This restaurant served truckers, so it was actually open at the predawn hour.

We slipped into a booth and ordered coffee and omelets from the tired, middle-aged waitress and I got a side of bacon. We didn't talk much, both of us keeping an eye out, but it was just the one waitress and a few truckers, the hiss of cooking food in the kitchen wafting in with the smells, mixing with the sounds of trucks and the faint whiff of diesel fuel.

No one here was living the dream, we were all just getting through another day, getting ready to put in more miles or working to pay the bills.

"Any emergency and we turn and fly away," I said to Licia when the food was most of the way gone and my hunger was no longer screaming in my ear. "We don't give them any time. We go fast and straight up."

She nodded, her tired brown eyes finding mine. "And the interview?"

I shrugged. "I think we have to take on one problem at a time."

Her mouth twisted into a frown, which she tried to cover up by taking a drink of her coffee. I could hear, loud and clear, what she hadn't said. Dealing with one problem at a time, Project Vulcan in particular, is what got us into this mess.

"Okay," I said with a nod. "That hasn't been going so well. What do you think our next step should be if that happens?"

"Anything else for you two?" the waitress asked. Her name tag said "Harriet." She had a simple wedding band on her left hand and her grey hair lay flat against her head. She was tired. I doubted that she would remember us, just two more bikers taking a break from the road.

"Apple pie, if you have any," Licia said with a smile. "A la mode for him. And the name of a decent place to crash."

"You got it, hon," she said, plodding back towards the kitchen.

"Switzerland," Licia said once the waitress was out of earshot. "Or Thailand. Hell, I don't care. If we go up, we come down fast in a country that will welcome us."

Suddenly the clanking of dishes in the back was loud and the squeal of a semi's brakes put me on edge.

Licia had a pained look on her face and I understood it. Completely. "Leave the country..." I mumbled.

She nodded sharply, sipping more coffee.

For her to even suggest this was... it was nothing short of desperation. I was an only child, but she had a big family, cousins, seemingly, everywhere.

Our parents, while all still alive, were getting old, all of them approaching their eighties. We had talked to them a lot at Casita de Soledad and once or twice a year Homeland would let them come visit. We had assurance that we would be able to leave—escorted of course—in case of medical emergencies.

Leaving the country meant leaving our parents to live the ends of their lives without us. I mean, that had obviously changed with setting off the bomb, but this made it real, way too real.

And another layer of guilt descended on me. I hadn't given them one thought when I was so desperate, feeling so trapped.

"Here you two go," Harriet said, setting the pie down in front of us. "Best place in town is the Green River Inn. It's on the main drag, right on the river, you can't miss it. Tell 'em Harriet sent you."

And then she was gone and I was staring at the apple pie, watching the vanilla ice cream slowly melt, the food I had already eaten feeling like a lead weight in my stomach.

Licia reached out and grabbed my hand and squeezed it. She didn't say "I'm sorry" or "I love you," but I could feel both.

It dawned on me that she had been so silent since our escape partially because she had figured this out way before I did.

"We... we can't leave them," I said looking up from the pie to Licia's compassionate brown eyes. "Everything else, but you, I can let go of, but we can't just leave our parents."

She nodded and sniffed, her eyes moist. "So let's get back on the road and get closer to that interview."

Licia pulled out enough cash for the meal and we walked out into the lightening sky as dawn approached. "What about that motel?"

Licia shrugged as she put her helmet on. "Just in case, to throw them off the scent."

I got on the Harley behind her and it roared to life. No more thoughts of sleep. We needed to get somewhere where it would be easier to hide. No turning. No flying away. We had to get to that interview.

FALL 2006, THE ATLANTIC OCEAN

I OPENED MY EYES AND SAW SWIRLING GREY AROUND ME. There was very little light and the dark grey shapes gave me a greater sense of motion which just made the vertigo worse. On top of my starved, dehydrated state, that was just too much and I closed my eyes again, breathing shallowly.

I was under the water, but there was air around me. It didn't make sense, but then again, very little had in the last few years.

It was hard to track time. I was so exhausted that I fell asleep as I was swept along in my bubble of air, that watery sound becoming lulling as I got used to it.

As consciousness returned, I heard the watery sound again, but it was much more normal. Water flowing and sloshing. I wasn't moving anymore, and I could sense light through my closed eyes.

I slowly opened my eyes, blinking against the brightness. I was... well, there is no easy way to explain this, and many of you may doubt this, but like everything I've told you it is true.

I opened my eyes and found I was still in a bubble of air, still under the water, but dappled shafts of light flowed down through the deep blue water. A movement to my right caught my attention as a pod of dolphins swam by and I swear they were looking at me.

I was floating... somehow... in the middle of the air bubble that was, maybe, thirty feet below the surface. I could see the waves playing with the light above me. A thin tube of air extended from the bubble up to the surface, providing me with fresh, cool air.

I was no longer in a nor'easter. I was no longer freezing cold. The sleep had refreshed me, but I was still very dehydrated—my head spiking with pain—and starving.

A dolphin came close, straight towards me with something dangling from its mouth. She poked her nose through the air bubble and dropped a small rubbery bag into my hands before chirping and backing out of the bubble and just staring at me as if she was asking me whether I was going to open it or not. The dolphin was a she, I was sure of it.

Thoughts of Aquaman and Doctor Dolittle came to mind. I didn't know it yet, but I was not, bizarrely, that far off.

The bag was made of rubberized nylon with a top that rolled down and clipped together. It was some kind of dry bag. A school of small silvery fish swam by as I opened the bag. Inside were two water bottles and a ham and cheese sandwich. A dolphin had just delivered me lunch.

I shrugged and smiled, still in the parka the policewoman had given me, figuring if I was in a dream, I might as well enjoy it. I sipped the water and slowly ate the sandwich, not wanting to overdo it with my much-abused body. And I watched the show.

Dolphins swam around me, schools of fish swam by in the distance, below me were craggy boulders on the sandy floor of the ocean with fish darting in and out.

I wasn't in the tropics or anything, but after all that I had just been through with the airplane, it was pretty wonderful.

When I had drunk all the water and eaten the food, my body starting to revive a bit, she appeared.

Well, really, she made an entrance. Dolphins had been circling me the whole time I had been there, a pod of ten or twelve. The first thing that happened was they shot off quickly as if something had spooked them, or maybe someone had called them.

Soon they came back, an obvious gap in the middle of their formation and in that gap was... a swirl of dark, denser water. A shape. A presence. The form wasn't still enough to describe a shape, its size wasn't consistent either, but it was clearly there as if the ocean itself had taken on a watery form.

I bet this isn't making any sense. This is really hard to describe, but let me try again. If you've ever seen the water from above, warmer portions will appear lighter, you can see how it's not all the same depth or temperature, not all moving the same way. That was happening here, but much more intensely. The water the dolphins were escorting was much denser, probably warmer, light more reflecting off of it than going through it. It was water, but it wasn't the same as the rest of the water.

The dolphins came straight towards my bubble, splitting around it and the watery presence didn't turn but entered the bubble, becoming more solid as she approached. As the watery form came close, began to change, her feminine nature was very clear.

As her form became denser and more human, the dolphins swam swiftly around the bubble and then more joined them and all I could see outside of the bubble were the sleek grey forms of the dolphins.

But my eyes were on her. As her form became more human, I saw that she was tall with graceful, athletic limbs and long seaweed-green hair that flowed in sheets covering her breasts. Her eyes, though, were blue like the waters of the Caribbean.

"Hello, Nik Nichols, the one they call Neutrinoman. He that is the fire to my water," she said, extending her hand. "It is high time we met. I am Neptuna."

SUMMER 2025, DENVER, COLORADO

WE STAYED ON I-70 UNTIL WE GOT TO GRAND JUNCTION, Colorado. As the sun rose, the road got busier and the miles stacked up. We didn't talk much, there wasn't much to say. Licia focused on driving and I kept a lookout, every time I saw the highway patrol or the police, my heart thumped in my chest.

They were looking for us. They had to be looking for us, even if Jean and Alan hadn't said anything. It began to bother me that we weren't meeting any opposition or having any close calls.

It was just Licia and me on the Harley, my butt slowly going numb.

At Grand Junction we headed southeast, opting to get off the highway in favor of smaller roads. It would slow us down, but we hoped there would be fewer watching.

The forests and the little towns and the miles all blended together with our fatigue. We stopped for gas, caffeine, and quick food. Me, I would have survived on chips and hot dogs, but Licia insisted we eat fruit smoothies and simple things like bagels.

Seven hours later, early in the afternoon, we hit Denver, both of us too weary to put together a coherent sentence. The I-25 corridor south from Colorado Springs, through Denver and north to Fort Collins, is a dense stretch of humanity, the cities much like any other except for the looming Rocky Mountains to the west. We headed north and got off the highway and headed towards Henderson and picked an old motel at random. Licia checked us in and then we stowed the Harley at a park a few blocks away and stumbled back and passed out on the old brown-and-orange toned bedspread of the queen bed.

Sleep. We had to sleep. There was no choice.

This wasn't the romantic Chinese food and fun that Licia had promised in the storage unit in Fredonia several states and a thousand miles ago. This was our fatigue growing large enough to take over our desperation.

The plan, or more honestly put, the hope, was that we would be very hard to find in the middle of this metropolis. Anonymity was our shield, whether Jean had told the cops about us or not. Whether the military was looking here or not.

I woke up with a start, drool pooling on the bedspread below my face, the hum of the city alarming me after waking up for so many years in the middle of nowhere.

I looked around and Licia walked out of the bathroom, her long black hair wet and a white towel around her torso offsetting her olive skin. She looked better, but still tired.

"We have to leave the Harley," she said.

My brain wasn't working yet. For a moment I was just waking up to see my beautiful wife just out of the shower, a most happy way to wake up, and then it all came back in a rush and I groaned.

"I know," she said, thinking my groan was about leaving the Harley, but I hadn't processed that yet. I was groaning because of the mess we were in.

I pushed myself up, still fully clothed, my hand going to my cheek and the imprint of the bedspread's fabric that was there from not having moved for so long. My stomach was growling, my bladder full, and my mouth was dry. I looked at the clock and it said 8:02—I must have been out for sixteen hours.

She sat down next to me with a sigh and I took her hand.

"I'm sorry," I said. My butt would love to leave the Harley behind, but I understood. It would be like me leaving my dad's Dodge Charger behind. That Charger, by the way, he was still tinkering with it and hadn't fully restored yet all these years later.

She gave me a wan smile. "We'll leave it where it is and hide the key around here. I've got a second cousin close and I'll send him a postcard, so maybe..."

She didn't finish. She didn't say that maybe someday we'll be in a position where she could get it back, because that just didn't seem possible today.

"We buying a car then?" I asked.

She shook her head. "Buying a car with cash could draw some attention."

"Then what?"

"Amtrak," she said with a whisper of a smile. "We get a sleeper compartment and don't come out until we get to Chicago."

I nodded. There was risk. In every direction there was risk. We could be recognized. I grabbed the remote from the bed, pressed the microphone icon and said, "Play WNN."

The TV came to life and on the screen was a female anchor— I didn't watch much news and wasn't familiar with her. She was blond and perfectly quaffed in that oh-so-plastic way. To her left were photos of Licia and I, not very flattering ones. Licia's was an overexposed picture of her some paparazzi got off at night with a flash in which she looked ghostly white. Not flattering. My picture had me with my mouth tight as if I was about to yell at someone, probably the guy who had shoved a camera in my face. The choice of those photos told you a lot about what they thought about us.

"...source exclusive to WNN say there is direct evidence that the attack on the Nichols/Lopez compound was alien in nature."

"Compound?" That had a sinister ring to it. Maybe my books hadn't made the kind of progress I had hoped... or maybe it was just making the divide in opinions greater.

The image switched to an overhead view of our former home with the eerily round scoop taken out of the desert, like some giant ice cream scooper had come down and carved it out.

"Where are Nichols and Lopez?" the anchor continued. "Are they still alive? Agent Peters with Homeland Security had this to say yesterday evening."

The view switched to Peters, his bald head shiny in the sun, sweat running down his cheek, the desert laid out behind him. "We have found no evidence of Nichols or Lopez," he said, swallowing hard. "We don't know what caused the blast and we don't know if they lived or died. There's nothing..." he looked off into the distance, his eyes haunted, before clearing his throat again and continuing. "There's nothing left. Not one trace of any of the buildings, any of their possessions, or them."

"Bastard," Licia growled at his lie. She had been kind to him for many years.

The image switched back to the blond anchor. "Does this mean the end of Neutrinoman and Lightningirl? Stay tuned to WNN for around the clock coverage of this breaking story at the top of every hour."

Licia grabbed the remote, turned the TV off and stood up, her arms hugging her chest. "Shit!"

We had been so focused on escape we had—if we had even been thinking about it—assumed Homeland would cover this up, that it wouldn't be a huge news story. We didn't expect them to get ahead of the story, lay down their own narrative. We didn't think everyone in the world would like being reminded again of exactly what we looked like.

Shit!

"There goes our interview with Diane Madison," I said.

And then it occurred to me that Byte and her drones were the reason for this ground they were laying. They knew someone knew about what had happened, so they were establishing the story before we could.

Once again, this all felt like my fault.

FALL 2006, THE ATLANTIC OCEAN

SHE WAS BEAUTIFUL, WITH HER FLOWING GREEN HAIR, LITHE limbs, full lips, youthful features, and piercing Caribbean-blue eyes. But then again, goddesses should be beautiful. Lightningirl, goddess of electricity, or perhaps ether if you're thinking in traditional terms. Gaia, goddess of the earth, and now Neptuna, goddess of the sea.

But the name... "Neptuna" was... it just seemed off to me. Too much like the fish "tuna" or maybe thinking that a goddess's name shouldn't just be a small tweak to the Roman god's name.

I shook her hand, her grip strong, but not in a showy way. "Hi..." I began. I mean, what do you say to a naked woman who, somehow, has transported you through the ocean, has created you an air bubble so you can breathe, and had a dolphin deliver you lunch. "I'm sorry. I feel like you know a lot about me, but I've never heard of you."

The sound in the bubble was echoey and strange, a constant gurgle of water in the background.

"Yes," she said with a pleasant smile, "and let's keep it that way, shall we. My friend, Byte, who commands all things technological, is the only one, besides you now, that knows of me."

Well that helped put some things into place, like the magical water runway and the wave that helped take the 787 to shore. Byte had a way to communicate with her. Also, Toxicwasteman's puzzlement over all of it and Byte's dramatic "don't try to follow me" exit into the ocean. He didn't know about Neptuna.

She didn't have an accent, not really, but she put together words in an odd way. "The fire to my water," "who commands all things technological." It was almost as if she was a queen and used to addressing her subjects.

"Then why did you bring me here?" I asked.

"You gather the heroes, do you not?"

I nodded. "Heroes Incorporated. We are preparing to meet the alien threat."

"Thus our meeting," she said, gesturing to me and the water around us. The dolphins still swam all around the air bubble as if they were guarding her.

"You want to join?" I asked.

"Well, Mr. Nichols, I believe I already have, helping you and the chemical man land that plane."

Something wasn't right. Byte was on that plane, and while Neptuna did help, I was sure it was about Byte.

And then it hit me. The name.

"Can I ask you a question? It will help me in understanding if you are the type of q-morph we are looking for," I asked. Yes, she clearly was a q-morph, an elemental like Licia and Tom and myself.

Her smooth brow furrowed but she said, "Ask me anything!"

"Your name, 'Neptuna.' Can you tell me how you came to be called that?" Her eyes narrowed and her brow furrowed even deeper. "I know it's a weird question, but I've found it helpful in illuminating the person behind the name."

She folded her arms, her head cocked and she stared at me. I was taking a risk, I knew that. I might have recovered enough to turn briefly, but if I was far out to sea, I wouldn't be able to make it to land. I might be the fire to her water, but I had only a spark left and we were surrounded by water. It would really be best not to make her angry.

"This ain't working, is it?" she asked, her lips pursing, her skin darkening slightly, her face transforming into something that looked Asian and about ten years older. I'm embarrassed to say I couldn't really tell you if she was Chinese or Japanese or Korean. I blame it on growing up in the Desert Southwest of America. Her voice changed to, gone was the regal tone, and while it was mildly accented, I couldn't tell you what Asian country it was from. "Byte, she said this might help, throw you off my identity, but she also said that you weren't dumb."

I just blinked, not knowing what to say.

Neptuna got a sheepish look on her face. "The name... well, my daughter's five. She came up with it." She ended with a shrug. "She also came up with Waterwoman, Seagirl, and Fishlady. So you might see why I went with Neptuna."

I smiled.

"So, am I in?" she asked, a cheerful look on her face. "My identity really does need to remain a secret, you'll have to communicate with me through Byte, but... well, I can do some stuff."

I nodded, still processing. That landing had certainly been "some stuff."

"You know I helped Tornado with that hurricane a couple of months ago." She leaned close and got a conspiratorial look on her face. "Don't tell him, the delicate male ego and all, but isn't he dreamy?"

Now it was my turn to furrow my brow. "Delicate male ego." Was that a cut at me? After all, she had brought me, and effectively trapped me, here. And that comment was sexist to boot.

"See, right there," she said gently. "That's your delicate male ego at work. I can see it on your face."

"Umm..." I only spoke because it seemed like I should be saying something, but I had absolutely nothing to say. I mean, I am well aware of being male and having an ego and egos in general being very delicate things.

"Not that women don't have egos," she continued. "We do, believe me. It's just that... well, look around, Nik Nichols, this world is run by men, and women are still constantly objectified and earn much less than men. And that's in the developed world. Forget about how women are treated in the rest of the world. So yes, while we have egos, they have become strong because of all that we have had to go through. I stand by my statement. Don't tell Timothy Tran, the Tornado, that I helped him. Delicate male egos and all."

She paused and the gurgle of water seemed louder than it had before. I got what she was saying, but I have to say that my delicate male ego did not like it at all.

"So am I in?" she asked with a bright smile.

FALL 2006, THE ATLANTIC OCEAN

NEPTUNA HAD RULES. PARAMETERS. SPECIFICALLY, HOW AND
when she would participate in Heroes Incorporated. Always
anonymously. Always through Byte. Always in ways that did not
involve her appearing physically like she was to me right now in
that gurgling bubble of air under the ocean with the dolphins
circling us.

I began to doubt that I was even looking at the real woman with
her Asian features and hint of an accent. The royal Neptuna was a
ruse, this likely was too.

But I didn't really care. She had immense power and it could be
useful to Heroes Incorporated and doing our paid jobs. She could
cool ocean temperature enough to blunt hurricanes and change
their paths. Tornado would be the above ground, the visible source
of the work, but she would be below the waves doing even more.

And we would protect Tornado's "delicate male ego," true, but
it was mostly about her anonymity. Here was a q-morph that even
Tom Tyree didn't know about. Although with what we saw getting

that 787 to the beach, he has to suspect, but that was Byte's problem, not mine.

Actually, it's not either of our problems, because he turned himself in and he had much, much bigger fish to fry.

"I have several conditions," I said with a smile which I hoped was charming, but I still was clothed only in a winter parka and a few thin airline blankets. I was still undernourished and dehydrated.

"Conditions?" she asked, her head tilting and her eyes narrowing. That royal air of hers was certainly not gone, there was some truth to it. And I guess if you can control the oceans and talk to dolphins you might feel kind of special.

"Yes," I said. "I think they will be simple for you to provide."

She made a casual rolling gesture with her hand as if I were a servant and she was impatient for me to get to the point.

"One, since Byte is how I communicate with you, I am assuming you can guarantee her wholehearted participation in Heroes Incorporated."

Puzzlement passed across her face, but only briefly, as if she had believed that Byte was already wholeheartedly a part of Heroes Incorporated. Which made me wonder, again, whether this whole plane thing wasn't some kind of setup, but I wasn't believing Tom Tyree was behind it all anymore.

"Of course," she said with a confident smile. "Anything else?"

"I need you to find Gaia and bring her on board," I said.

"Gaia?"

I smiled, not buying her feigned innocence. She said she had a daughter, and I believed her, which meant she had a life above the waves. Everyone saw the footage of the seven-hundred-foot-tall rock giant that destroyed the Hoover Dam. Everyone knew about Gaia at this point. She wasn't a very good liar, and I liked that about her.

"The earth to your water," I offered.

"Oh yes... of course," she said. "We have not met. I am not sure how I can help you there."

I sighed and nodded. "Very well. It was really good of you to help with getting that plane to the ground. You saved a lot of lives." I looked around as if I was in a conference room looking for the door. "I really should get back to the plane. I'm sure the authorities have some questions for me."

She sighed and nodded. "I can't guarantee her participation, but I can arrange a meeting with her for you."

"Thank you," I said. "And can you at least get her to stop her activities until we talk? No more earthquakes, no more sink holes."

She shrugged. "I will try."

"Thank you." I extended my hand. "Welcome to Heroes Incorporated."

"THEY'RE PLANNING ON KILLING US," LICIA SAID AS SHE PACED the worn brown carpet of our Denver motel room.

I nodded. The conclusion was pretty inescapable. Agent Peters —whose life we saved along with the rest of the Homeland agents who had been spying on us by making them evacuate—was laying the groundwork, convincing the world that we were already gone.

The only sliver of a doubt was that he was just covering his own ass and not acting on orders. But that was just a sliver, there were a number of other agents in that base that all knew what really happened.

If they found us, they could kill us and no one would be the wiser. It would be an alien attack on Casita de Soledad that did it, not the bullet from a Marine. A nice clean end to the difficult task of keeping us around.

And I could—almost—see their point. If we resurfaced, if we convinced the world it was the military's Project Vulcan, a use of alien technology, that they had created in violation of the Accords, it wouldn't go well for them. Byte had evidence of our survival, of those soldiers trying to capture us after the incident.

It wasn't enough evidence, not really, but enough to show that they were lying about what had happened at Casita de Soledad.

As Licia paced, I stumbled into the bathroom, took care of my urgent needs, drank a bunch of water, and got into the shower. I let the hot water pound on my head, hoping it would wake me up, but my thoughts were disorganized. It was just too much. Too many things arrayed against us with nothing on our side.

Byte had helped us escape, she might be able to help us survive, but she wasn't exactly my greatest fan anymore. She, like everyone else, only wanted to keep me around just in case the aliens came back.

But would that be enough? And, besides, I was frankly sick of being kept around like that. A weapon you lock away and bring out only in dire circumstances.

"I've got it!" Licia cried as she ripped the shower curtain back.

I squinted at her, soap in my eyes. "We need Byte," I said, tentatively, my thoughts not yet clear.

"Yes!" she said, her voice loud. "And we need to bring back Heroes Incorporated."

My jaw dropped. I was just thinking about using one of the online drops I set up with Byte to have her figure out how to get us out of the country, but this...

I cleared the soap from my eyes and smiled. "This is going to be so dangerous," I said, seeing a glimpse of what she was talking about.

She nodded, a gleam in her eye and a wicked smile on her face.

"We need Jean and Alan to talk about what we did," I offered, finally catching on.

"Oh, yeah," she said, a smile lighting up her face. "And we're keeping the goddamn Harley!"

"We'll need a semi, I think, and some support staff," I said, my brain finally engaged. This was a little bit the Incredible Hulk and a lot the former Heroes Incorporated.

Licia smiled widely. "We'll probably go down in flames."

I shrugged. "At least we'll be fighting for a good cause."

And then the tears were running down her face and I knew it wasn't because she was scared, but because she was relieved. This new Heroes Incorporated would be a fly-by-night, low-key, vigilante-type operation, but we could help people and the world would know that Neutrinoman and Lightningirl were not dead and gone. God only knows how Homeland will spin that, but one step at a time.

She was crying because now we could actually do something, actually have a life, actually use our abilities to help people again. It wasn't the freedom we needed to be with our families, but it was a lot more freedom than we've had, and maybe, just maybe, a step towards a normal life.

I grabbed her and pulled her into the shower and ripped that towel off of her. She giggled and I kissed her hard.

Time to embrace our powers and not run from them anymore. Time to be heroes again.

FALL 2006, THE ATLANTIC OCEAN

I NEVER WANTED TO BE A TORPEDO, SLICING THROUGH THE water at a blinding pace. After Neptuna was done talking to me—and that is exactly what it was, this royal dismissal—she said, "Best get rid of that parka before the water hits." And then I was suddenly horizontal and moving fast, the dolphins making room for me as me and my bubble of air headed out into deeper water.

I watched, but not for too long. The bubble became smaller, occasionally joining with other air bubbles that I ran into, refreshing my air as older air was released and floated to the surface. I saw fish and sharks and then nothing as the bubble headed into deeper, darker water. The speed, it was dizzying, and I was still a complete mess despite the water and sandwich the dolphin delivered. I squeezed my eyes shut and just wished for solid land.

This time the ride lasted less than an hour and suddenly the bubble was gone and I was deep under water, the pressure hurting my ears, the parka sucking the water in and weighing me down.

The water was icy, sapping my strength as I struggled with the parka, got it off, and started swimming up.

Neptuna had taken me from the shore, why couldn't she deliver me there? Was this another whiff of her royal manner, did she want to prove her power over me?

When I bobbed above the surface, I sucked in cold air, a sandy shore and sand dunes beyond. This wasn't Long Island. Where the hell was I?

The cold was numbing as I started to swim, unsure I had the energy to get to shore, fairly sure I didn't have the energy to turn into Neutrinoman and fly to shore. So I swam, the water gently swelling underneath me, turning into waves and then breaking ahead.

The salt stung my eyes, but the effort helped with the cold water. It wasn't warm here, by any stretch, but there was some blue in the sky amidst the high clouds and I clearly wasn't in the middle of a nor'easter.

I did fairly good until the waves started crashing on me, pushing my head under, shoving the saltwater up my nose, and just as I started to panic, strong arms grabbed me.

"I got you, brother," my rescuer said. His voice was deep and he had an odd, vaguely European accent.

"Quinn?" I sputtered.

"At your service!" he said, way too enthusiastically. He put me on my back, his arm over my chest and started swimming strongly for the shore. I was exhausted and let him.

"I'm here, Nik. I'll always be here," he said, and in my desperation and exhaustion it didn't sound the least bit creepy.

I was soon coughing on the shore, the dregs of the waves washing over me, and I got a good look at Quinn Rask. He was 6'4" and muscular with jet black hair and blue eyes. He was also as naked as I was.

"How?" I spat out, panting.

He shrugged, an elegant gesture, his breath easy as he sat on the sand.

"A woman with an English accent called me, said you would need some help. Told me to get here. Aren't you glad to see me, Nik?"

I did my best to smile and nodded. "So glad, Quinn." I crawled a little farther towards the dry sand. "Where is here?"

"North Carolina."

Quinn got up, jogged to the dry sand and brought back a towel and helped me get up. He was still very naked, and given his abilities, I'm sure not the least bit cold. I was having a hard time keeping my shivering down.

"Www... When did the woman call? What time?"

He shrugged. "I don't know, about four hours ago. She told me exactly where to go."

The sun was getting low on the horizon and I did the math and realized that he had been called before the mysterious runway had appeared. My encounter with Neptuna and my deposit here several states away was all planned.

Byte and Neptuna had planned it.

Up the beach, Quinn had a blanket laid out with a bunch of power bars, bottles of water, and clothing for me to wear. "She said you would be hungry," Quinn said when he saw my eyes light up. "You look like feces, by the way. What happened?"

I grabbed a water bottle and nodded at him. "Put some clothes on and I'll tell you."

The click-squish sound of Quinn using his powers to change his appearance gave me the usual queasy feeling and soon he looked like he was wearing a black tuxedo.

"Nice, but that's not clothing," I said.

"You hurt me, Nik," he said. "I save your life and again you reject what I am with your stupid American prudishness."

I shook my head. He appeared to be clothed, but it was all him, his flexible form looking like clothing now. In my mind he was still as naked as he'd been when he rescued me, but I didn't have the energy for this old argument.

I put the clothes on and told him the story while I devoured the food and water, while he sat there relaxed in a freaking tuxedo.

"What happened to that robot?" he asked at the end. "The one that attacked you from the landing gear?"

My mouth dropped open. I had completely forgotten about it. I had no idea. I shook my head and washed down my third power bar with some water.

"Okay," he said nodding his head. "Alien robots attack plane. Byte helps you become the engine and discover beast mode so you can keep it in air. Toxicwasteman joins at end, but day really saved by mysterious underwater force. Toxicwasteman turns himself into authorities. Alien tech robot gets away. You are mysteriously transported here. And, it now appears that Byte may be in charge of LoVE not Toxicwasteman. Did I get it all right?"

I nodded slowly. I hadn't told him about my meeting with Neptuna and told him I wasn't sure how I ended up down here. He wasn't completely buying that, but him laying out what had happened in the last few hours left me breathless.

He patted me on the back. "This has been a good day for our little enterprise. I was listening to the news on the way in. They are talking about how you saved the plane and convinced Toxicwasteman to turn himself in peacefully. What's next, boss?"

Good day? Sure, hundreds of lives were saved which does make it a good day, but what about Neptuna and Byte? It's clear that Byte arranged much of what happened, but did she know about the robots in the first place? And if so, how did she get them, and was she actually working for the aliens?

I shook my head. I couldn't believe that. I saw Toxicwasteman destroy an alien ship in Yellowstone, his animus towards the aliens was not an act. Byte couldn't be in league with them, she must have just used the attack opportunistically to push me further—and to survive.

"Well?" Quinn asked, staring at me. "Tiger got your tongue?"

I smiled at his mangled idiom and took a deep breath and looked around. The cold beach was deserted. "How did you get here? Do you have a car?"

He nodded and pointed towards some steps that led between a couple of sand dunes.

"I need a phone," I said. "We need to see if there is any sign of that robot. I'll need to brief Colonel Williams. I want to check on Licia." I pushed myself up, and the beach started to spin and I would have fallen, but Quinn caught me.

"I got you, Nik. What I think you need is Jennifer Johnson. She'll know how to make you not so skinny."

I nodded and let him help me up the beach.

There was a lot to do yet. More heroes to recruit. A base to build. So many preparations to make.

But right then, what I needed was a nap.

FALL 2006, AFRICA

THE GOOD NEWS WAS THAT THE AIRLINE THAT FLEW THAT 787 that we saved was so grateful that they became a sponsor of Heroes Incorporated and provided us with gratis flights around the world.

The bad news was... all those flights around the world.

When Byte transmitted Neptuna's message that Gaia wanted to meet in Africa, it's not like I could claim that the flight was too expensive and couldn't we just meet in Arizona somewhere... or really anywhere within the continental United States that I could fly to easily under my own power.

Add onto my prison-induced phobia of small spaces, the fear that any flight would soon be sabotaged by some morphing silver alien robots and I would be forced to push myself way past the extremes to save it.

I don't think you can call that paranoia. I mean, those little robots *were* out to get me. The military *had* imprisoned me. The aliens *were* out there deciding the fate of our planet.

I can report, though, that beside my low-grade panic attack, the flight was very long, quite boring, and without incident. Licia held my hand. Valentine Oscar, my self-appointed bodyguard, sat calmly and stoically, having made it quite clear that after the incident with the 787 he planned to never leave my side.

Nevertheless, I was more than glad when the jeep driver dropped us off in front of a large expanse of African savanna. He looked at us, his eyes wide, and he said, "No farther. This land, it is hers. No farther."

So comforting.

Yet there was sky above us, the ground below us, grasslands sweeping away to the horizon dotted with those umbrella-shaped acacia trees, and a small herd of zebra in the distance.

"What now?" Licia asked, adjusting her backpack.

I nodded towards the zebra. "We walk south, we're looking for a cone-shaped upthrust of rocks."

"She's messing with us, you know," Licia said.

I nodded and smiled, still glad to just have my feet on the ground. "I don't blame her," I replied. "Our encounter at the Hoover Dam didn't exactly go well."

"Damn Hammer," Licia growled.

"Quinn is working on a less aggressive version of the Hammer," I said.

Licia just shook her head. There were stories there, stories of the time when Quinn posed as Neutrinoman while I was in prison. Stories Licia still hadn't shared with me. What with the recovering from the trauma, breaking from the military, and the Heroes Incorporated madness, we hadn't had time.

I glanced at Val, he had binoculars out scanning the landscape. "No rocks in sight," he said. Val was taller than me, an athletic middle-aged man with short grey hair and sharp pale blue eyes.

"So let's walk," I said, happily striding out into the savanna in search of Gaia, goddess of the earth, the last q-morph elemental we needed for Heroes Incorporated.

———

GAIA WAS MESSING WITH US. VAL WOULD SPOT AN ODD stacking of rocks on the horizon with his binoculars, we would hike towards it for an hour, maybe two, and then it would be gone.

The day was hot, but not oppressively so and it wasn't an unpleasant way to spend the day. We spotted elephants and giraffes, I heard some roars that I suspected were lions, but no wildlife approached us.

I'm sure we were an odd sight for the animals. Humans out here were generally in jeeps, and in larger groups ready to defend themselves against the wildlife.

With Licia here, I wasn't worried. She could suck electricity from any attackers. We avoided the termite mounds and watched for snakes, and let Gaia lead us on a circuitous route deep into the savanna.

Towards the end of day, as low mountains were becoming visible on the horizon, we finally reached an odd upthrust of rock. My feet were sore, my clothing sweaty, but I was actually happy. No board meetings. No decisions made. No dire emergencies faced. I'd spent the whole day with Licia and we had enough time for our conversation to wander away from the immediate madness on to simpler things. The kind of common intimacy that couples often fall into but we just hadn't had the time for.

Val fell back and gave us space when this happened. We held hands and talked quietly. We laughed. She told me that she really wanted a dog... or moreover, a life that could properly support a dog. A house and a place to walk the dog. A schedule that was normal. A simpler life.

I told her that sounded like heaven and hugged her on the African grassland for a long time, no longer caring about today's particular mission.

It was then that Val spotted the rock upthrust, this time closer than before. Gaia had been watching us, obviously, maybe even listening. I wonder if that interchange Licia and I had was why she finally let us find her.

When we got to the rocks, I was a bit disappointed that it was over, or at least I thought it was. The rocks were just that, rocks. Tan boulders naked of vegetation rising up about thirty feet, roughly cone shaped and forty feet in diameter at the base and about ten feet in diameter at the top.

This didn't look natural, but there was no sign of Gaia and the rocks didn't move.

"Look," Val called from the other side.

Licia and I walked over and saw what he was pointing at. There was a slice of this thing made of smaller rocks and formed what was clearly a staircase winding up to the top. The staircase wasn't cut into the rocks but was made up of smaller rocks.

"She's messing with us," Licia said again, but this time with a smile on her face.

I nodded. "I can't say I mind."

"You can't go up there," Val said mildly. "It could be a trap."

I shrugged. "Val, my friend, it's all a trap. But I don't think she means us any harm."

I got on the first stone step and extended my hand to Licia.

———

GAIA WAS THERE, OF COURSE. HER NAKED SKIN A DEEP BROWN in the waning sunlight, her feet buried in the soil of the flat top of the rocky upthrust. Her eyes met Val's when he got to the top and she slowly shook her head, her lips forming a thin line.

"We'll be okay, Val," Licia said, putting a hand on his arm. "Wait for us on the ground."

His eyes narrowed as he assessed the naked woman and the rocks she had so easily assembled with her thoughts. He had seen the video of the rock giant she was when she wrecked the Hoover Dam. She was clearly a threat to us, and to him, but still you could see the calculation in his eyes as he weighed the risk.

Val was a different kind of man. I was not his boss, he had no boss, really. He was here on his own because he felt this was the best way to contribute to the war against the aliens. I had come to trust him and appreciate his calm presence.

He smiled at Licia. It was thin and brief, and I swear his body looked more poised for action than usual. That smile wasn't of resignation, it wasn't an admission that he could do nothing to us powerful q-morphs. That smile was a calculation that Gaia didn't mean us any harm.

After he made it to the ground, Gaia spread her hands, palms up and said, "My friend Neptuna said you wished to talk. I hope that we are not rudely interrupted this time."

I smiled because this was a different kind of greeting from her. More Jena Grange than Gaia.

The elements are thought of differently by different traditions, but for us q-morphs it is: Gaia is the earth, Neptuna is the water, Lightningirl is electricity, Tornado is air, and I am fire.

Five elementals. Six if we add in Toxicwasteman and the element of chemicals, provided he is out of jail by the time this all happens.

If we could work together, if we could combine our powers, it seemed to me like that would have to be enough to defend this planet. To give humanity, as flawed as it is, time to sort its problems out.

EPILOGUE

THE ARIZONA HIGH DESERT SUN HUNG IN THE WASHED-OUT blue sky, a light breeze licking at the sweat on my forehead, my breath coming fast and my mind calm at the end of a long run.

As I gazed past the busyness of Ruby, Arizona, and the under-construction home of Heroes Incorporated at the craggy upthrust of Montana Mountain, I couldn't help but think of Gaia. We spent three days talking with her. At night she would descend into the ground and Val would come up and be with us as we made a simple camp safely on the top of Gaia's rocks.

For a long time, the three of us elemental q-morphs talked as friends might talk. About our pasts and our doubts and our fears, and even our dreams. We were just Jena, Licia, and Nik. And then on the last day we talked about Heroes Incorporated and the exis-tential threat that the aliens posed to all of us.

Gaia wanted to also talk about the existential threats of climate change, deforestation, species going extinct, human rights viola-tions, and all the other challenges facing our world.

These were not easy conversations. I wanted her on our team and she wanted us on her team.

We were preparing to fight the aliens and she was trying to save the planet... all of it, not just taking on this single threat.

We made plans, we set things in motion, including taking ten percent of the Heroes Incorporated seed money and starting a nonprofit. But it wasn't clear how any of it would play out yet. Would Gaia be with us when the fight began? Could our little nonprofit really do much good against the huge problems that faced us?

It was a lot. All of it. Too much, really.

The ever-present sound of construction equipment beeping brought me back to the Arizona desert. The sound was starting to get on my nerves, especially the beep-beep-beep of heavy equipment backing up.

I was finding, and this was no surprise to anyone, especially not Licia, that I was something of a hands-on leader.

Heroes Incorporated had purchased Ruby, Arizona, a ghost town southwest of Tucson and four miles from the Mexican border. This put me close enough to Palo Verde Nuclear Generating Station if I needed to charge. It also put us close enough to another country in case things got weird with the US government again.

Ruby sits in rolling high desert hills near Montana Mountain at four thousand feet elevation with two small lakes and a flat area of old mining tailings that remind me of Groom Lake in Area 51. This made Ruby spotable from orbit, another plus. Two UH-1 helicopters, on loan from the military, sat on the far end of tailings next to a fuel tank.

Ruby was a mining town, once the home of the Montana Mine that pulled gold, silver, lead, and more out of the ground. There's old mine shafts, schoolhouses, a mercantile, and more buildings on the property in various states of decrepitude.

Some of these have been torn down, making way for the large

concrete building with a large circle-H symbol on the side and a flat roof.

It looked nothing like a superhero base in the movies would look like. Heroes Incorporated has money, but this is about speed and economy. The building was a hulking rectangle made out of bland, grey, concrete slabs. It will contain offices and workspaces. It sits next to a smaller version of itself which was setup a few months ago and right now Jennifer Johnson was transforming it into our medical facility.

At the near end of the tailings flat, just below Town Lake (which, this being Arizona is more the size of a pond) mobile homes were being put in place for housing and near it a new well was being drilled and large septic tanks were being put in.

The rattling hum of a generator mixed with the noise of the construction. APS was in the process of getting more power to us, but that would take time. We had several wind turbines planted on the hilltops and solar panels on every available roof, but Licia needed all the power she could get.

It was a strange sight. I was on the north end of Ruby, on the recently widened dirt road taking it all in, pulling in deep breaths, dressed in shorts, recovering from a long run on the dirt roads around here.

I always stopped to look at the rapidly changing tableau when I got back. One of my rare moments of stillness. Somehow all the new buildings seemed to fit right in with the buildings from the past, a new boom town that will fade back into obscurity before too long.

It's not that I was pessimistic or anything, it was just reality. We would either win the war and Heroes Incorporated would not be needed anymore, or we would lose and... well, none of us would be left.

Our newly minted, Gaia-inspired nonprofit was based in Phoenix. We were housing the hero operation out here because we needed the room and the privacy, and we feared direct alien attack and didn't want to be near any population centers.

Valentine Oscar was standing next to me, his knees bent, his eyes scanning the landscape. He was dressed in his usual black, running shorts and a T-shirt this time, his short grey hair bright in the sunlight. I've had a hard time convincing him to leave me since the incident with the 787, not that he could have done much in that crisis. He took his self-appointed job of bodyguard very seriously and never let me out of his sight. He was quite a bit older than me, but a better endurance runner and had been helping me clean up my sloppy form.

I tried putting Val on the payroll, now that my father had the accounting department up and running in Phoenix, but he wouldn't hear of it. He said, "I don't need the money and I will not sully this effort with something so base."

There was more to it, though, I was sure of it. Since he was on no payroll, he had no one to answer to but himself, and that is what he wanted. I admired his position, and it put into stark contrast the hundreds of millions of dollars being given to fund Heroes Incorporated.

Down on the flats, I could see a glint of red hair as a woman did a lot of pointing, instructing some of the workers. My mother had taken it on herself to run the HR department and anything around here that has to do with quality of life. She's a redhead now, something I haven't gotten used to yet, but it was good to have her here.

Quinn was with her in his Hammer-light form carrying things, tweaking the position of trailers, doing whatever my mother told him. This was a smarter, not quite as strong version of the Hammer that caused such a mess at the Hoover Dam. I smiled as I watched. He stepped first one way and then the other. I could just imagine my mother telling him to do three things at once.

Near the crane as it lowered in another concrete section of the new building stood a short, broad-shouldered man in a yellow hardhat. John Lopez, Licia's father. He was directing the construction effort and his wife, Elena, was organizing the kitchen, currently a cluster of food trucks down on the tailing flats near the trailers.

And yes, we took a lot of heat about nepotism when the media found out, but frankly, I didn't care. I still don't. We needed those that we trusted close to us, as many as we could get.

But I worried about the danger, not just for our parents, but for the q-morphs assembled and everyone else. The different types of danger. Not just the Arcturian Alliance, but the growing backlash from q-morphs doing damage when they were helping people or the intensifying media scrutiny and the paparazzi that assailed us whenever we were in the real world.

Like the lawsuit filed against me concerning the damage to Las Vegas when the remnants of the meteor hit. Or the rumblings from the United States Bureau of Reclamation about the cost to rebuild the Hoover Dam. Heroes Incorporated had money and that changed everything, and often not in a good way.

We had a team of lawyers on the payroll and those kinds of costs just rubbed me the wrong way. That meteor had been a planet killer, the pieces that had gotten through were nothing compared to what it would have done. If we hadn't been at the Hoover Dam, Gaia would have completely destroyed it and who knows what else.

We had to convince the world that things were much better with us here, thus the PR department working out of Los Angeles.

My rumination continued. This new life was a lot more stressful than before the break with the military, trying to balance getting the enterprise up and running with all its myriad of details *and* thinking about how we deal with the aliens if they come back.

I wasn't a janitor anymore with a simple job that I could leave behind after the end of the workday. It was all meetings and reports and conference calls. Plus training, public appearances, and the occasional operation.

This hadn't left much time for Licia and me since our trip to the savanna a few months ago and that had been bothering me more and more, but of the many problems I had, I hadn't been able to figure that one out.

She was on the Heroes Incorporated board of directors, so she had to sit in on plenty of meetings and read some of those boring reports, but she was spending a fair amount of time out in the field doing the kinds of money-generating jobs we needed done for the income, and for the good will it produced.

When the military was in charge, I hated being kept in the dark, now... I longed to know a lot less.

Val's phone beeped and he looked at it. "Diane Madison and her escort have left the Tucson airport. They'll be here in approximately ninety minutes."

"Very good," I said, nodding.

"Excuse me, but do you think this is a good idea?" Val asked. "She is the one that revealed your identities and has been relentless on breaking news about you."

I sighed. "Of course I'm not sure. But what is that old saying? Keep your friends close and your enemies closer. We need to let the media further in. We'll see how she does."

Optics. Public perception. Appearances. All of these things drove me crazy. What we needed to do was focus on the job of keeping the human race alive, not focusing on the latest news cycle and what the world thinks of the latest half-truths the media is serving up about us.

But I was naive then. In retrospect I think this all would have gone better if I had spent more time focused on the optics.

I chuckled as I watched my mother have the Hammer move a new trailer back to the exact same position it used to be in.

Val's phone chimed again. It wasn't really the role he wanted, but since he was with me most all the time, he served as something of an assistant. "Ms. Lopez has requested a few minutes of your time down on the flats. She wishes to meet you there in five minutes."

I smiled, and we started down the dusty road towards the mine shaft and buildings. This issue that Licia and I faced felt big. We were trying to save the world *and* be in love at the same time. But I knew, for the most part, it was the challenge that all couples face. How do you take care of life's voracious needs for your time and have the space and focus for intimacy and connection and love? And, no, I'm not talking about sex... at least not just about sex. Physical intimacy, in general, is a lot more straightforward than emotional intimacy, a lot easier than finding the time to beat back the urgent and just talk with your partner.

We walked past the construction site and I waved at Mr. Lopez who gave me a curt nod in return. Frankly, I didn't think he was happy about this enterprise, and the danger to his daughter. I had pondered reminding him that she was in it before we met, but I didn't think that would help.

Beyond the building was the renovated mine shaft with steel girders and a working elevator instead of a rickety wooden contraption. Gayle Smythe, our head of IT, and I am quite sure not Byte's real name, insisted on this. We have some underground storage and some emergency shelters built in the old mine and our servers are being installed down there.

She wasn't here much, she conferenced in for meetings, and spent more time in our Phoenix offices where a lot more servers were located.

Licia knew who she really was, but no one else did.

Tom Tyree was currently being held at Luke Air Force Base. I'd visited him a few times. This was a whole thing between the military and me. They wanted to put him in the facility at Area 51 and I had to threaten breaking ties to stop them. I demanded that the remaining q-morphs there be released, but they told me there were no other q-morphs, despite the evidence I saw of it during my stay.

The world didn't know about that facility, and they really couldn't yet, but I'd be damned if I'd see someone else thrown into that hole. That prison was firmly in the "Deal with later" column of my extensive to-do list.

The road ran next to Town Lake (really it was just a pond) under the thin shade of some mesquite trees and onto the flats. We had the tailings tested, thoroughly, and it was a boon to have this large, flat area for our temporary buildings.

Licia was standing there smiling like she was a kid with a secret she just couldn't keep anymore. It made me smile. Her long black hair was pulled into a ponytail and she had on khaki shorts and a white tank top.

She was so beautiful. More beautiful than when I met her. And you all might be getting tired of me saying how beautiful she is, but it's just a fact. I will admit, though, that the more I know her, the more I see her strength and her heart, the more beautiful she becomes.

As I write this, Licia looks, maybe, five years older than she did then. I imagine when enough time has passed to counteract the anti-aging effects for our q-morph transformations, when she is wrinkled and truly looks old, I will still find her just as beautiful. Different, yes, but still beautiful.

Isn't that the way it should be? The years change your love's appearance, but if you are lucky, they are still your love and you've found a way to stay together and stay intimate through all those changes.

"Come on," Licia said, taking my hand, a glint in her eyes. She gave a pointed look to Val who got the hint and hung back.

Mom waved at me from a few trailers away and the Hammer gave me an exasperated nod, but I was focused on Licia. She was excited, walking fast, a spring in her step.

She took us through the twenty or so trailers there to one on the edge of the flat with a hearty juniper that was growing at the edge of the tailings. She smiled and nodded at the trailer, beaming.

I smiled back, but I didn't quite get it. It was one of the many single-wide trailers set up here, painted grey with some metal steps leading up to the door. It wasn't anything special. I mostly slept in my office, which was a horrible habit, but Licia had been gone a lot lately and there was so much to do.

"Really?" she asked, letting go of my hand and crossing her arms.

I was tired. Clearly she had done something nice and really wanted me to notice it. I took a step back and really looked at the trailer, letting my breath deepen and slow. I hadn't been making enough time to meditate and I really needed to do that.

The living room window had some blue curtains and I could see that electricity, water, and sewer connections were complete, the pipes and the wires snaking down in the tailings.

There was a simple wooden sign on the door with names engraved there. Each trailer had one, so you could tell them apart.

This one said "Lopez / Nichols."

My heart started beating hard and there was no chance of meditation anymore. Was she saying that...?

"Are... are we living together now?" I asked.

She looked away, suddenly shy. "If you want to."

I swallowed hard. I was in prison for six months, and then the long recovery, and the recruiting, and the 787 and recovering from that, and building Heroes Incorporated. When we were together, we stayed together, but we never had a place, "our" place.

When I blinked back tears and sniffed she looked back at me, tears pooling in her eyes as she nodded.

This, right here, this is what I wanted. I wanted her to be front and center and the world and all its problems to be second. I wanted to do simple things like plant a garden together, get that dog she so wanted, read the paper over leisurely breakfasts.

I didn't talk. I grabbed her and pulled her off her feet in a fierce hug. I didn't have the words.

"Come on," she said after I put her down. "Let's go look at our house."

Tears flowed down my face as she showed me *our* house. I felt no shame for more tears, only love for Licia and hope. This here, this is what could keep me together while the madness raged. The world and all its demands wouldn't go away, but this tiny sanctuary with her would give me strength to do what needed to be done, to endure the meetings and the media and all the demands of Heroes Incorporated. To help find a way to defeat the aliens. This would be enough.

It had to be enough.

EPISODE 7

HEROES INCORPORATED

THERE IS MORE ADVENTURE, MORE FUN, MORE *NEUTRINOMAN and Lightningirl* coming soon in episode 7, *Heroes Incorporated.* Sign up for my newsletter at RobertJMcCarter.com/newsletter and don't miss a thing.

And for the same kind of romantic adventurous fun as *Neutrinoman and Lightningirl* set in post-apocalypse Arizona, check out *Woody and June versus the Apocalypse.* Join the fan club at Woody-AndJune.com and get the first two episodes for free!

▭

WOODY AND JUNE VERSUS THE APOCALYPSE

Love and the Apocalypse

When Woody Beckman meets June Medina, neither expects the adventures that will follow. Dedicated go-it-alone survivors, they've learned not to trust anyone in post-zombie-apocalypse Arizona.

But when regular-guy Woody must save tough-as-nails June, they realize that to survive they must learn to trust each other.

As the pair deals with everything from zombies to psychotic, petty, wannabe warlords to the harsh Arizona deserts, they start to realize that they might just prefer facing this crazy world together.

A story of adventure and love and taking things (even the apocalypse) in stride.

Get the first two episodes for free by joining the fan club or go grab Volume 1 with all 7 episodes!

Robert J. McCarter is the author of seven novels, three novellas, and dozens of short stories. He is a finalist for the *Writers of the Future* contest and his stories have appeared or are forthcoming in *The Saturday Evening Post*, *Pulphouse Fiction Magazine*, *Fiction River*, *Andromeda Spaceways Inflight Magazine*, and numerous anthologies.

His latest effort is a serialized novel called *Woody and June Versus the Apocalypse*, a story of adventure and love and taking things (even the apocalypse) in stride. Of his novel, *Seeing Forever*, Kirkus Reviews says, "Sci-fi as it should be: engaging, moving, and grand in scope."

He lives in the mountains of Arizona with his amazing wife and his ridiculously adorable dogs.

Find out more at:
robertjmccarter.com

BOOKS BY ROBERT J. MCCARTER

NEUTRINOMAN & LIGHTNINGIRL: A LOVE STORY

- Meteor Attack!
- Toxic Asset
- Protocol X
- Season 1 (Omnibus edition of Episodes 1 - 3)
- Off Book
- Hard Times
- Elemental Factors
- Season 2 (Omnibus edition of Episodes 4-6, coming August , 2020)

Find out the latest at Neutrinoman.com

WOODY AND JUNE VERSUS THE APOCALYPSE

1. Woody and June versus the Wannabe Warlord
2. Woody and June versus the Fungus-Head Zombies
3. Woody and June versus the Grand Canyon
4. Woody and June versus the Ex
5. Woody and June versus the Third Wheel
6. Woody and June versus Phantom Company
7. Woody and June versus the Daring Rescue
8. Volume 1: Episodes 1-7 (all seven episodes for a great price)

Join the Woody and June Fan Club at WoodyAndJune.com

For a complete list, go to RobertJMcCarter.com